Praise for *Murder in Lascaux*, the first Nora Barnes and Toby Sandler Mystery

"This densely written and marvelously detailed excursion through the Dordogne will leave you dreaming of castles, chateaus, and caves."

Library Journal (Starred Review)

"A whodunit that nicely balances a breezily light travelogue with urgency and suspense. Readers will hope this is the first of a series."

Publishers Weekly

"With a colorful mélange of art, French history, food, and a surprising perp, this tale will keep readers entertained (and entice them to visit southwestern France)." *Booklist*

"Crisply written. . . . If you like a murder mystery you can get your teeth into, give this one a try." *Mystery Scene Magazine*

"A strong first mystery that tells a traditional amateur detective story in a fascinating setting." *Chicago Tribune*

Praise for *The Body in Bodega Bay*, the second Nora Barnes and Toby Sandler Mystery

"Colorful characters . . . keep the proceedings fresh and unpredictable. . . . The unexpected but satisfying conclusion is worth the wait."

Publishers Weekly

"If you're a fan of Alfred Hitchcock's *The Birds*, you will thoroughly enjoy this murder mystery that takes place in Bodega Bay, the town where the scary avian movie was shot." *Mystery Scene Magazine*

"Betsy Draine and Michael Hinden must be having a wonderful time researching and writing their mystery series. It certainly is a lot of fun reading their books."

Capital Times

"The prose is elegant and the plot beautifully researched."

San Francisco Book Review

"Nora Barnes and Toby Sandler are back. This crime's solution takes us into the world of Russian icons, the Russian past in Sonoma County, and even into the realm of communications from guardian angels. *Murder in Lascaux* was an auspicious debut; *The Body in Bodega Bay* continues the journey. This novel delivers. Grab it and enjoy."

Richard Schwartz, author of *The Last Voice You Hear*

Praise for *Death on a Starry Night*, the third Nora Barnes and Toby Sandler Mystery

"Making their third sleuthing appearance (after *The Body in Bodega Bay*), Nora and Toby are utterly delightful. . . . Mystery devotees who want an atmospheric crime novel with an art history slant such as Iain Pears's 'Jonathan Argyll' books will enjoy this series."

Library Journal

"Into the mix of personalities, the authors weave in tantalizing snippets of letters written by Isabelle's grandfather about his acquaintance with the extremely moody and vulnerable Van Gogh in 1890. The result is an entertaining whodunit."

Alfred Hitchcock Mystery Magazine

"Highly recommended and certain to be an enduringly popular addition to the personal reading lists of mystery buffs."

Midwest Book Review

"A rich and colorful novel that sometimes seems almost as real as the history it's based upon. . . . Readers who cherish France, fine dining, classic art or simply a smart mystery will find plenty to enthrall them in *Death on a Starry Night*."

Isthmus

The Dead of Achill Island

A Nora Barnes and Toby Sandler Mystery

Betsy Draine and Michael Hinden

The University of Wisconsin Press

The University of Wisconsin Press
1930 Monroe Street, 3rd Floor
Madison, Wisconsin 53711-2059
uwpress.wisc.edu

Gray's Inn House, 127 Clerkenwell Road
London EC1R 5DB, United Kingdom
eurospanbookstore.com

Printed in the United States of America

This book may be available in a digital edition.

Library of Congress Cataloging-in-Publication Data

Names: Draine, Betsy, 1945- author. | Hinden, Michael, author.
Title: The dead of Achill Island / Betsy Draine and Michael Hinden.
Description: Madison, Wisconsin: The University of Wisconsin Press, [2019]
| Series: A Nora Barnes and Toby Sandler mystery
Identifiers: LCCN 2018045767 | ISBN 9780299323806 (cloth: alk. paper)
Subjects: | LCGFT: Fiction. | Detective and mystery fiction. | Novels.
Classification: LCC PS3604.R343 D425 2019 | DDC 813/.6—dc23
LC record available at https://lccn.loc.gov/2018045767

To the Irish side of the family

The Dead of Achill Island

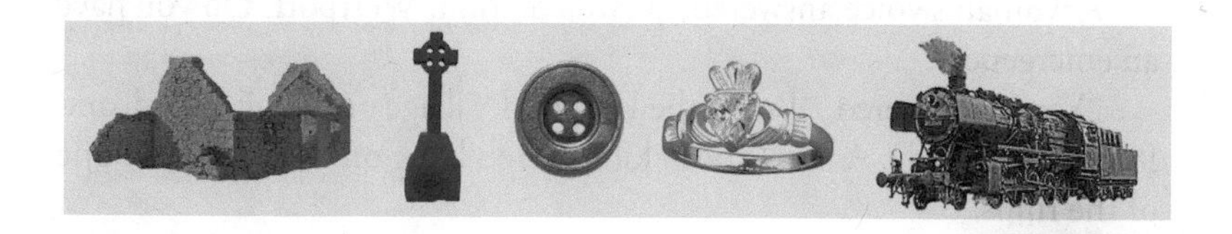

1

THE BODY WAS SPRAWLED FACEDOWN on the grass floor of a roofless cottage open to the sky. The head was a tangle of gray hair and drying blood, and more gore was smeared on a nearby rock. The ruin where he lay was one of a row of stone hovels that stretched across the foot of the mountain. Wind howled through the chinks of broken walls; there was no other sound. Bending down, I felt his neck but found no pulse.

God help us, we're rid of him at last.

I stood and scanned the slope, cupping my eyes against the morning sun. Close and far, the rubble of a hundred houses weighed upon a line that extended the length of Slievemore Mountain. Above the row of houses, the slope rose quickly to pale, rocky heights.

I turned toward the sea and saw no one on the hill below me, only a few sheep in the graveyard near the entrance to the Deserted Village. I was the first visitor of the day—except for him. I took a long look at him and then closed my eyes. Eventually, I opened them and then retched at the sight of the mangled head. A shiny object on the ground next to his chin caught the sun and startled me. I stared at it, hoping I was wrong. I picked it up, put it in my jacket pocket, and fumbled for my phone. There was no point in delaying further.

A woman's voice answered, "Garda Station, Westport. Do you have an emergency?"

"Yes," I answered. "I'm at the Deserted Village on Achill Island, and I've found a body. A man's been killed. He's lying on the ground in one of the ruins."

"Mother of God. Hold on," she said. "I'll put you through to Achill Sound."

It took a while to make the connection. I repeated my message. There was consternation in the voice that replied. I heard the squeaking of a chair and pictured a rural policeman pushing back sharply from his desk. A moment's pause; then came a barrage of questions.

"Your name, please."

"Nora Barnes."

"B-a-r-n-e-s?"

"That's right."

"You're not from here?"

"No, I'm American."

"Are you staying on Achill?"

"Yes." I gave him the location of our holiday cottage.

"You're saying there's a dead body at the Deserted Village. When did you find this body?" He sounded skeptical.

"Just now. A moment ago."

"And where exactly are you?"

"I'm at one of the first houses up the hill from the entrance gate." I thought I heard the scratching of a pen.

"One of the ruins. Are you sure, now, this man is dead?"

"I am. He isn't breathing."

"Right. You said he was 'killed' when you called the emergency operator. What made you say that? The poor man maybe had a heart attack, I'm thinking."

"Sir, his head's bashed in and there's blood all over."

"Jaysus," said the officer. "You haven't touched him or moved him, I hope?"

"Just to feel for a pulse. He doesn't have one."

"Well, you're not to touch a thing from now on, you hear? I'll call the detectives and be there myself very shortly. Wait for me, will you?"

"I will."

"One more thing. Do you know who the dead man is, by any chance?"

Oh, yes. I knew who he was, all right. "His name is Bertram Barnes," I said. "My uncle." Uncle Bert, the bastard.

That's what my mother called him. She rarely mentioned his name without the epithet. We kids liked the sound of it, so that's what we called him too.

"Your uncle? Why didn't you say?" I didn't reply. He continued, hesitantly. "Well, could be you're in shock. I . . . I'm sorry for your trouble. Just stay where you are. I'm on my way."

Ten minutes later I saw a car, a white sedan with GARDA painted in blue across the hood. It slid to a stop in the dirt parking area for visitors. I was sitting outside the ruin that contained Bert's body. I stood and waved to the officer as he hustled up the hill carrying a clipboard. While he climbed, I scrutinized the ground, looking for footprints. The grass, moist with morning dew, was thick and tightly rooted. I wondered if it would take a footprint. I couldn't make out my own, never mind the killer's. Maybe the officer would see something I couldn't.

He was young, with soft features and a pink complexion. Pudgy rather than fat, he was clearly winded from the climb. He wore a light-blue shirt with black epaulettes and navy pants. The tightness of his uniform stiffened his movement as he knelt beside the body, studying the bloodied head and making notes. Then turning to me, he said he was Garda Matt Mullen of the Achill Sound station. The inspector, he said, was on his way from Westport to take charge of questioning me, since there was evidence of a violent crime. A technical team would be dispatched from Dublin to gather forensic evidence. His job was to secure the scene and to keep an eye on any witnesses or suspects until his colleagues arrived.

"Are you all right?" he asked solicitously. But I could read his mind: Which was I, a witness or a suspect? Whatever his doubts, the young garda was polite. "Would you like some water?" He extended a plastic bottle. "At the station, I could have offered you a cup of tea, at least."

"No need," I replied.

"There's just the one of me, you see. I'm meant to have another guard with me, but she's on maternity leave. I'm on my own." He glanced at the sky. "At least the day is fine, so it won't be too hard on you waiting outdoors. But the Crime Scene Technical Bureau will want a tent over the building for when it rains, so I've got work to do." He motioned for me to sit on a pile of stone rubble close by, and he returned to where the body lay. While I watched, he wound yellow tape around the ruined house and its lifeless guest.

Waiting for the inspector, I ran over the events of the past few days. Our trip had started out full of promise. I was with my parents, my younger sister, Angie, and Toby, my husband. We had come to Ireland to honor Dad's cousin Bridget. It was her Silver Jubilee, her twenty-fifth year of being a nun. Celebrations in Galway began with a Mass said by Bridget's brother, a monsignor who had come over from the states. Two of Bridget's ten siblings read from the Gospels and the Epistles, and a fellow nun gave tribute to Bridget's worthy service of twenty-five years.

The party afterward felt like a silver wedding anniversary, and in a sense it was, except that the husband was missing (or in heaven if you believed in it). No anniversary party ever had livelier dancing, both before and after the meal. I was stunned to see a group of nuns stepping in unison to a country-and-western line dance. As for us, we danced passably and took hasty breaks for drinks. It was a wonderful evening of family fun; that is, until a set-to between my mother and Uncle Bert marred its end.

We tried to put that bitter scene behind us as we set off after the party for our holiday on Achill Island. Achill (it rhymes with "cackle") is Ireland's largest island. It lies off the northwest coast above Galway and is now connected to the mainland by a causeway. "Why don't you go up to Achill afterward?" Bridget had written to me before the trip. "It's still unspoiled. The Brits, you know, did their best to stamp out our culture. But the West was too poor and too far from England for them to bother much about, so it's where the old ways are best preserved. And Achill is about as far west as an Irishman can get."

Taking Bridget's advice, we arranged a holiday on Achill, hoping to get a feel for the land our grandparents left. Bridget found two small cottages for us to rent, one for Mom, Dad, and Angie, and one next door for Toby and me. For months ahead, I daydreamed about the party in Galway and the ten days the family would have on Achill Island, soaking up the atmosphere of old Ireland.

It wasn't until the Jubilee dinner that we learned Uncle Bert would be on Achill at the same time, in connection with one of his real estate projects. The cottage he was renting was in walking distance of our own. Had we known that earlier, we would have made other plans. It didn't take a conspiracy theory to conclude that Cousin Bridget sent us to Achill knowing that Bert would be there and hoping there would be a reconciliation. Her intentions were the best, but you know what they say about the road to hell.

I looked toward the ruined hovel, where the guard was working around my uncle's body. With the face hidden and the form inert, already somehow shrunken, the corpse didn't much resemble the man I had known. That man held himself high with his chest puffed out. He strutted like a major general, issuing commands in a booming voice. Even at funerals, he would shatter the quiet of the room. He was larger than life. But no one is larger than death.

When we were young, Dad would put my brother, Eddie, to bed and Mom would settle me in. For Mom and me, it was a time for confidences. One night she talked about Uncle Bert. It was the first time I heard her use the word "bastard."

"The bastard is as rich as Scrooge McDuck. And just as selfish."

"Does he sit on piles of gold?" I asked, thinking of my comic books.

"He sits on piles of shit."

That's the first time I heard her use that word too. I must have shown little-girl shock, because I remember that she shot back: "Don't look at me like that! The man's a shit and he makes his money in shit." I knew it was a bad thing to say, but I didn't understand how anyone could make money that way.

As I got older, our talks got longer and went deeper. I came to understand what she meant. Uncle Bert made his money in real estate. He bought and managed slum housing in Boston. He kept hundreds of people in poverty, overcharging for rent, evicting some tenants who missed a payment, lending money to others in ways that indentured them, letting buildings run down until they were so derelict that even the poorest of the working poor wouldn't live in them. They moved out, and drug dealers and squatters moved in. The decay spread, and soon a whole street looked ready for the bulldozer. But that's not what Uncle Bert sent in. He sent builders. He sent renovation teams. He received accolades for "saving the neighborhood." He reaped a fortune by gentrifying. Nobody gave a damn about the people displaced after years of exploitation, nobody but Mom.

I wondered what Dad thought about his brother's business, but the topic didn't come up, because Dad didn't talk about Bert. It was as if he didn't exist until, once or twice a year, he would stop by unannounced (or so I thought). I came to realize that Dad did know he was coming and quietly alerted Mom. She was always in the bedroom reading when he arrived, and she let somebody else answer the door. Bert and Dad would go off by themselves to Dad's basement workshop or for a walk outdoors. A few hours later, Dad would reappear, and nothing would be said about Bert's visit, but Mom would avoid Dad's eyes.

Every year or so, there was a funeral or christening in the extended family. Bert would make his rounds of the room, clapping the men's backs and kissing the ladies' cheeks. When he got to Dad, the brothers would have a chat. It was the only time Bert used his "indoor voice" and I couldn't hear what he was saying. Sometimes Mom would glance at them, looking sour. My brother called it her witch face.

We rarely saw the witch face. Ordinarily Mom looked more like Cinderella. She worked hard at home and at her job, and her labors kept her lean. Lipstick was the only cosmetic she wore, and her dark, wavy hair, styled by nothing but air-drying and a hairbrush, fell loosely below her shoulders. She wore the same boatneck tees and white jeans all year long. There wasn't a day in her life when her clothes and jewelry together cost more than thirty dollars. But to me she looked beautiful, and when she laughed it made me happy.

If fury possessed her, it was always about Bert. It's strange how, in a family, you fail to ask questions about the things that most disturb you. I sensed that Uncle Bert had done something worse in Mom's eyes than make a dirty million, something more personal that hurt her, or us, directly. But I didn't dare ask.

It came out after a Christmas dinner at Grammy's, our annual attempt to be a united family. My new cousin, Emily, had been in the family three years, since her mother's marriage to Bert. She was a year older than I was, and much prettier. I tried to be her friend, but she kept me at a distance by talking incessantly, so that there was no time for friendship. That year she talked on and on about her vacations to places like Bermuda, where her new family had a bungalow, and to Paris. Her descriptions left me envious. When we came home, I asked Mom why I couldn't go to Paris and Bermuda like Emily. She said nothing, but her jaw set and it seemed to me she was tamping down a fire inside. I thought it was my fault; I was being jealous and greedy. "I'm sorry," I said. "I don't really want to go to Paris."

She took my hand and said, "Sweetheart, you deserve to go everywhere in the world. But our family is different from Emily's."

"You mean, they're rich and we're poor?" I asked. "Is it because Dad's a postman?"

She dropped my hand and stepped back. "There's nothing wrong with being a postman, Nora. Your father works hard and does an honest day's work." She paused but lost the battle against her anger. "That's more than I can say for your uncle. It's because of him that your father never went to college. Dad's twice as smart as Bert."

"Then why didn't Dad go to college?"

"Granddad saved up for it, and Dad did too. He wanted to go to UMass, like his friends. So he worked two jobs, one after school and another on the weekends, but Bert pulled the rug out from under him. Bert's the one that went to college. And he used Dad's money to do it."

I pictured Bert finding a stash of money under Dad's bed and taking it for himself. That would be really sneaky. Just to make sure, I asked, "How did he do it?"

"He's a con man, that's how, and he's always been one. He pulled the wool over the eyes of some naïve teacher—got her to convince Granddad he was a genius and they had to send him to a fine university. The teacher tutored him through his junior year and got him into Boston College. She helped him do his applications, including an essay about how he came from poverty: immigrant parents, his father just a garage mechanic, blah, blah, blah. It was a snow job."

"But isn't Dad older than Uncle Bert? Why didn't Dad go first, and then Uncle Bert?"

"That's what should have happened. Even though Dad was a year ahead of him in high school, Bert convinced Dad to turn over his own savings and go to work to help put Bert through college first. Bert claimed that with a degree from BC, he could earn enough money to pay for Dad to go to college, help Granddad buy the garage, and even pay off the mortgage on the family home. Well, Dad put off college and never got another chance to go, and Bert got his golden ticket to the high life. And guess what? He never did a damn thing for your father. If I use bad language about him, now you know why."

I went to bed left with the knowledge that Dad had been cheated and our family had paid the price. That's why Dad was a postman and I couldn't go to Paris and why Uncle Bert was a bastard.

With that understanding, I made it my habit to avoid Uncle Bert. So I wasn't pleased that Cousin Bridget seated our two families together at the Jubilee dinner. The place cards put Dad opposite Bert, Mom opposite Bert's wife, Laura, and me opposite Cousin Emily, with lucky Toby and Angie paired at the end of the table. Years of practice keeping our distance at social events provided us with survival strategies. Dad and Bert exchanged a few words after the champagne toast and then spoke mainly to their respective spouses. Emily and I did some catching up. She asked me about my work; I asked about hers. I was an art history professor in Santa Rosa, California, and she worked for Uncle Bert, managing commercial real estate in Boston. I was married, she was single. After so many years apart, we found it difficult to connect. There was more silent eating than normal. I drank more wine than I generally do, and so did Mom and Dad. He called the waiter over to get extra bottles for our table. Bert was knocking back whiskeys like a native.

I was relieved when the after-dinner dancing started and an Irish cousin invited me to partner him in a reel. Toby and Angie joined in, and we were caught up in set dancing for close to an hour. Exhausted at the end of a long round, I headed back to our table to fetch my purse on the way to the restroom. I saw Uncle Bert and Aunt Laura from behind. He was leaning back in his chair. Mom was half-standing, with one hand planted on the table, her arm straight as a pillar, while her free hand jabbed toward Bert's chest. Her tone was threatening. I halted, like a squirrel in the middle of the road, listening. I made out phrases: "you little bastard . . . stole from your own brother . . . not enough for you?"

Was she drunk? The thought unfroze me. I walked toward the table and tried to catch Mom's eye. She had only Bert in the grip of her gaze. "Mom," I said weakly.

"Go away," she hissed without looking at me.

I backed off slowly. Aunt Laura turned toward me, looking lost. With a slight hand movement, she pled for me to stay. I stepped away out of Mom's sight but stayed close enough to hear.

"And now you think you're entitled to keep the beach house on top of it! Well, you're not getting that house! It's as much Jim's as yours."

"Gloria," he barked, "you don't know what you're talking—"

Mom cut him off. "I know more than you think." She glanced at Laura, as if uncertain whether to proceed in front of her, but she couldn't hold back. "You may have the title to the house, but you got it by taking advantage of your father, same as always."

"Grow up," Bert said, at a volume fit for the stage. "I was the one who took care of him in his old age. He was sick and broke and he couldn't pay his bills."

"Lucky for you," Mom replied. "Gave you the chance to lend him bits of money and watch him go under. When you had him by the nuts, you took the title to the house."

Laura raised her well-manicured hand and said, "Gloria, dear, it's not our business, is it? You and I should stay out of it." She put on the sappy smile that had always repelled me.

Mom kept on. "For God's sake, Laura. By rights, that house should get passed down to all of our children. As long as their grandmother's still living in it, my family can visit there. But what happens when she's gone? I've heard you're redoing the kitchen, right under her nose. Couldn't you wait until she's dead?"

Bert darted his arm across the table and grasped Mom's forearm. "You don't talk to my wife that way!" he warned. He twisted Mom's arm, and she gasped. "Get hold of yourself, Gloria," he ordered. "I won't stand for—"

That's when Dad arrived, coming up behind Bert. He placed his palms on his younger brother's shoulders and said, "Cut it out, now." Bert immediately let go of Mom's arm. For the first time, I realized that Dad was taller than Uncle Bert, and Bert was intimidated. Was it Dad's strength, or was it Bert's knowledge that Dad knew the truth about him?

Dad took Mom by the elbow, but she wasn't finished. Leaning in even closer to Bert's face, she said, "You've always been a scheming bastard. If you get that house, I hope you die in it. I hope the roof falls in on your swollen head."

And now here was Uncle Bert, lying in a roofless ruin with his head bashed in. What would the inspector make of that? From my perch on the hillside of the Deserted Village, I could see cars approaching the crossroads. The sedan, it turned out, carried the detectives, and the van belonged to the medical examiner. When the vehicles reached the parking area, Garda Mullen stopped his work at the crime scene and skidded down the slope to meet them. By the time the detectives reached me, they had been fully briefed. Mullen returned to his work.

The taller of the two showed a wallet badge and introduced himself as Detective Inspector Kevin O'Donnell, then presented his colleague,

Sergeant Pat Flynn. O'Donnell had cloudy gray eyes set in a skull too big for the rest of his body. He was slim to the point of bony. His collar seemed a size too large for his neck, perhaps to accommodate a bulging Adam's apple, which bobbed as he talked. I guessed he was in his forties. Sergeant Flynn was younger, shorter, and broader.

Flynn began by asking, formally, for my mobile number, home address, the purpose of my visit to Ireland, my arrival date, and traveling companions. He already knew my relation to the deceased. Were there other next of kin? I told him about Bert's wife and daughter and where they were staying on the island. Flynn recorded my answers in a pocket-sized notebook.

Then the inspector took over. "So your uncle was a real estate developer, from Boston?"

"Yes, that's right. I think he was here on business."

"We're aware of that." The inspector exchanged glances with his sergeant and switched gears. "How close were you to your uncle?"

"Not close. We didn't see him very often."

"Was that because you lived far apart?" Inspector O'Donnell asked.

"Fifty miles, maybe. Our families just led different lives."

"Was there bad blood between you?"

"I wouldn't say that," I responded. I wouldn't if I didn't have to, I added silently.

"And when did you last see your uncle, alive?"

"That was yesterday," I recalled, "at our cousin Bridget's Jubilee." I described the circumstances.

"How did your uncle seem at the time? Nervous, fearful, worried about anything?"

"Not that I noticed." We had hardly spoken at the Jubilee, and the argument at Bridget's party didn't say anything about his general state of mind. So I shrugged. O'Donnell let seconds go by, then turned his eyes to Sergeant Flynn.

"I'd like to go over your call to the emergency operator," said Flynn, almost timidly. "What time do you think you found the body?"

"It was seven fifteen. I checked my watch."

Flynn's broad brow furrowed. "It was half seven when you phoned the emergency number. Why the delay?"

The question sideswiped me. "I don't—I didn't realize I waited that long."

"There's a phone record," said the sergeant. "The call came in at seven thirty-two."

"I guess I was so jarred that I stood there a while."

"I see," said the inspector. "When you rang emergency, you said that a man had been killed. You used that very word, 'killed.' You seemed sure of that." He paused, waiting for an explanation.

I tried to regain my footing. "As I told Garda Mullen, I could see damage to the back of my uncle's head. It was covered in blood. And there was blood on a rock lying on the ground."

The inspector's eyes narrowed. "So, you concluded that he'd been struck with a rock?"

"That was my first thought, yes."

"Any other reason?"

"No, just that."

Sergeant Flynn stepped toward me and asked the alibi question, "Can you tell me where you were last night and through this morning?"

"Yes. Last night we had supper in Keel—my husband, my parents, my sister, and I—and then we came back to our cottages. Toby and I are renting one next door to my parents and sister. We watched some television and went to bed."

"What did you watch, then?" continued the sergeant.

"We watched the Gaelic channel."

"You speak Irish, do you now?" asked Inspector O'Donnell. His thin lips pursed in disbelief.

"No, but there was a documentary on Irish music. It was the best thing on. It had subtitles in English." A faint smile relaxed the inspector's gaunt face.

"That sums up last night," I said. "This morning I woke up early, had a cup of coffee, and came out here on my walk."

"Did you pass anyone on the way?" asked O'Donnell.

"Not a soul. Just sheep."

He glanced over at the ruin. "We won't know how long the body was exposed until the State Pathologist gives us the time of death. Your uncle may have died last night or early this morning. Do you have any idea why he might have come out here at night?"

"No, not at night. But I suppose there's nothing unusual about a visit here first thing in the morning. That was my intention, coming early to avoid the crowd. I was hoping to have the village to myself."

The inspector acknowledged my reply with a nod. The Deserted Village is the best-known tourist attraction on the island. No one knows exactly when its ghostly homes were built, but they were abandoned in the 1840s when the Great Famine struck. It's an eerie site.

"Very well," O'Donnell said. "One final thing. Do you know of anyone who might have wished to harm your uncle?"

There it was, the question I had been dreading. It would come out soon enough, the fight he had with my mother and the things she had said to his face at the Jubilee. There had been witnesses—Bert's wife, for one. Well, they could find that out from her, not me.

"Not really," I said.

The inspector grunted and gazed toward the ruin, where Garda Mullen was securing the tent. "All right," said O'Donnell. "You're free to go for now. Remain at your cottage, though. I'd like you to write up a brief statement, just how you discovered the body and what you saw. We'll come by to get the statement after we've spoken to next of kin." He turned and strode back to the ruin. His partner gave me a solemn nod and hustled after his chief.

I unclenched my teeth. I hadn't given anything away. But had they guessed I was holding something back? Only I could hear my heart thumping against my ribs, but had they noticed my shaking hands? I reached into the pocket of my jacket and nervously fingered the object I had found next to the body. Of course I knew what it was as soon as I picked it up—a silver button, from my mother's sweater.

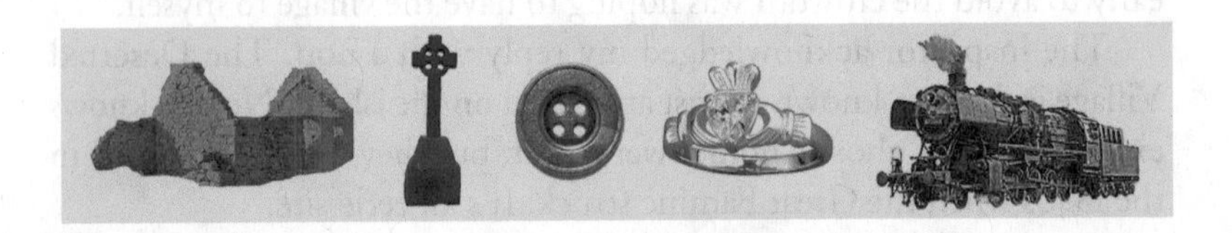

2

AS I JOGGED THE MILE-LONG PATH back toward our cottage, my mind was racing faster than my feet. Could my mother have murdered Uncle Bert? No, I wouldn't accept that. There must be another explanation. Maybe the button belonged to someone else. Buttons of that sort aren't unique. They're machine-made from some shiny metal, not really silver. Anyone wearing a wool cardigan like hers could have lost one, right? Maybe it had been lost weeks ago and had no connection with Uncle Bert, or Mom. That was possible, wasn't it? Tourists walked through the Deserted Village all the time. And yet.

My mother despised Uncle Bert. She tried to control her feelings, but sometimes she lost the battle. There was a crisis the year Aunt Laura tried to host the family Christmas in genteel Wellesley and Mom refused to go. The whole week before Christmas, Mom raged at Dad, sending Eddie and me out in the snow so she could have at him in private. We lived in Rockport, where the winters are cutting. Icy winds off the ocean blew us back indoors before she had finished, so we absorbed the heat of the argument and some of its sense. Mom refused to set foot in the grand home Bert had built with his father's money.

Compared to Uncle Bert's home, ours was a shack. Aunt Laura's one visit to us in Rockport made me feel ashamed. I remember her adjusting her skirt carefully on the roughened canvas of what we called the television couch. She seemed to be trying to avoid the stains of our family life. She looked at my mother with curiosity mixed with pity. According to Mom, Bert had told Laura that Dad was never a bright boy and had no ambition; he would always need somebody's help. "Bert claimed he got your father the job at the post office. And this disgusts me—he said your grandparents opposed our marriage because they thought Dad couldn't provide for me. Bert told Laura that he saved the day by promising he'd help Dad and me if we were ever in need. It was all a lie, just to make him look good and Dad look bad."

Mom hated Bert for demeaning Dad. Long before I knew the word "condescending," I sensed there was something wrong with the way Uncle Bert talked to my father. One time he came over when Mom was helping Dad lay linoleum in the bathroom. Bert made a show of marveling at Dad's DIY skills, lamenting that he had to keep a handyman on salary to do repairs and improvements on his house in Wellesley. He characterized the linoleum as practical and then complained that Aunt Laura insisted on Spanish tile. I could see Mom calculating the income difference between our family and Bert's. Every percentage of that difference was a sliver in her palm.

I loved Dad's gentleness, but I often wished he would stand up to his bully brother. Whenever Mom confronted him about this and other outrages, as she called them, Dad would remain silent, busying his hands with small manly tasks: draining the radiators, sealing a crack under a baseboard. Mom stood over him, forcing her argument, until he looked up, wincing, and said, "I know, Glo. It doesn't matter." The answer infuriated her. That's when she became the witch, flitting around the house with her face crabbed and tense. I was terrified when she was in that state, afraid that she would slaughter Dad, or Uncle Bert, or all of us. She never did, of course. But last night, in the Deserted Village, had her fury burst its reins?

I alternately jogged and trudged along the narrow road lined by high bushes that blocked all but glimpses of mountain on one side and fields on the other. If a car were to come by, there would be barely room to squeeze out of the way. I hugged the verge as voices competed in my head. Mom finally did it, said one. No, she couldn't have, said the other. I arrived at the turnoff for the Slievemore Cottages, carrying a weight of dread. It was an uphill climb to a plot of land dotted with small houses, but when I reached the top the ocean came back into view. The openness of the terrain, the morning sun, and the expanse of the sea returned me to clarity. It was up to me now to inform the family about Uncle Bert.

Our two cottages, identical in style, sat side by side, mine and Toby's and Mom and Dad's. They had been built for family vacations, and they were functional rather than charming: one story, whitewashed stucco on the outside with gray slate roofs. The door to ours stood open to the morning breeze. Toby was at the kitchen table still in his bathrobe, finishing his coffee. Even in his disheveled state, he looked appealing to me. "Hi there," he said, not lifting his eyes from the guidebook he was studying. I tried to respond, but my voice came out choked. He turned and asked, "What's up?"

"It's my Uncle Bert," I stammered. "He's dead." I spilled out everything I knew, in a torrent of words that subsided when I got to my suspicion about Mom.

"Whoa, hold on," said Toby, rising from his chair and wrapping his arms around me. His stubble scratched my cheek. "Don't jump to conclusions. You don't know what happened, let alone if your mother had anything to do with it. I can't picture her smashing someone's head in. Can you?"

He stepped back, still holding my shoulders, and gave me his "it can't be that bad" look. I wasn't to be comforted. "What about the button I found next to the body?" I protested. "I think it came off her sweater. And there's the fight she had with Bert at the Jubilee."

"A spat is one thing, murder is another. As for the button, it could be anybody's. The cops will sort it out."

I looked down at the floor.

Toby rolled his eyes. "You did give them the button, didn't you?" Pause. "Nora, didn't you?"

I produced the button from the pocket of my jacket.

Toby took it, held it in his open palm, and stared at it. He had something to say, and he was taking his time to prepare it. "This is wrong," he started. "It's withholding evidence. You could be arrested for it. Over here they call it perverting the course of justice."

I gulped. "You're not going to turn me in, are you?"

"Don't be melodramatic."

"Well, I'm not turning Mom in, either. She's my mother."

"You can't hide evidence from the police. Eventually the truth will come out, and then there'll be worse trouble than there is now."

"You said yourself, the button might not be hers."

"Yes. But the cops would try to trace who it belongs to, wouldn't they?" reasoned Toby. "If they knew about it."

There was a standoff, just a few moments, but it felt awful. I broke the silence. "The guards are coming soon. What are we going to do?"

"So it's 'we' now, huh?" Toby leaned his head sideways, pretending wariness. "Okay, it's 'we.' What we better do is find out as much as we can before they arrive. Let's go talk to your mother." He started moving toward the door.

"Like that?" I pointed.

"Hmm?" He looked down and realized that he was in his bathrobe, with nothing underneath. "Right. I'll get dressed. You, write that statement. Keep it brief and factual."

I didn't like being bossed around, but I knew I needed it, and I got the job done.

Mom and Dad's cottage lay across a gravel parking area that we shared. Their car was missing, but the door to their cottage was open. We found Mom in the front room of the house, a wood-paneled kitchen dominated by a large table and six chairs. She was at the sink doing the breakfast dishes. A man's barbecue apron covered the cotton robe she had bought on mail order from the Vermont Country Store. Even in that homely outfit, she looked as fresh as nature, ready to star in an ad for organic dish soap. "There you are," she greeted us, flashing her wide, welcoming smile. "Take a chair," she offered. "I'm making tea." The electric kettle was indeed growling and popping.

"Not for me, thanks," said Toby. "I've just had coffee."

"I wouldn't mind," I said. "Where's Dad? I have something to tell him, and you."

"Dad and Angie went to the store," Mom said. "They should be back soon." She dropped three tea bags into a family-sized teapot. "It looks like another beautiful day."

"Yup, we've been lucky with the weather," said Toby. He eyed me, as if to say, Go on. Get to the point.

"You have something to tell us?" asked Mom. I studied her face as she placed two mugs on the table. She looked her everyday self.

"It's bad news."

She started. "About Grammy?" My grandmother on Dad's side had stayed in Hull, in the beach house, nursing the pneumonia she had had for months.

"No. It's Uncle Bert. I'm sorry to bring the news. He's dead, Mom." Her eyes locked on mine. "I was the one who found him," I went on. "I was walking in the Deserted Village and saw him lying on the ground. The police are there now. I called them."

"What happened?" whispered Mom, her fingers covering her lips in a gesture of disbelief.

"I don't know. Maybe he fell, but he might have been assaulted," I said. "I saw blood on his head."

"Assaulted?" Her voice was cracking now. She sat down and closed her eyes. In a moment, she opened them and asked, "What about Laura and Emily? Do they know?"

"I'm sure they're being told," I replied. I wanted to say, You didn't do it, did you, Mom? But I couldn't bring myself to blurt it out.

"Your father will be devastated." She abruptly stood and went to the window. She swept her unruly hair back from her face, as if to see more clearly. Then she paced back and forth. "He'll be back any minute now." She slumped down on her chair again.

I poured the tea and doctored our cups with milk and sugar. "Mom," I said, "the guards are coming to get a write-up of my statement. They may want to talk to you. They'll be here soon."

"The guards?"

"The police," I said.

"Why would they want to talk to me?"

"Not just you. Everyone in the family," Toby clarified. "But you might start thinking about it, to get ready."

"What do you mean, get ready?"

"Just so you'll be prepared," I said.

"Why do I have to prepare?" she asked. She put her cup down harder than she meant to, splashing tea into the saucer.

"You did get into an argument with Bert at the Jubilee," I pointed out. "They're bound to ask you about that."

She made a little scoffing noise, looked down, and slowly shook her head. Then she raised her face defiantly and said, "Well, let them ask all they want. It's no secret I didn't like him, but plenty of others felt the same way. I'm not the only one." She thought for a moment. "It would be like Laura to blame me, though. What sort of questions do you think they'll ask, these guards?"

"For one thing," said Toby, "when was the last time you saw Bert?"

There was a moment's hesitation. "At the Jubilee, when I told him what I thought of him." She rubbed her knuckles in her lap.

"In Galway," said Toby. "Keep it simple."

"In Galway." She was looking at Toby, and her whole body seemed to be saying, Thank God—he's on my side. She took a sip of tea.

"And what about last night?" I probed. "You didn't go out or anything?"

"Out where? Where's there to go at night, around here?"

"Well, there are pubs," I said.

Her hands made a V in front of her face, a gesture that meant patience was running out. "If we were going to a pub, we would have asked you to join us, don't you think? We went to bed early. Angie did too. We were tired after the drive."

"So you were in all night after we came back from supper?"

"That's right. I might have stepped outside for a few minutes, to get some air, but I didn't go far."

Did I detect evasion, or was that my imagination? "And this morning? When did Dad and Angie go out, and have you been here all morning?"

"Of course I have. Look, I'm not even dressed yet. Angie and Dad went out about an hour ago, just over to the store." She turned toward Toby. "What else?"

"I don't know," said Toby. He looked at me. I looked at him. Neither of us had the nerve to say what was on our minds.

"Anyhow, why should I be worried about the police?" said Mom. "It's Dad I'm worried about. When he finds out about Bert."

"Do you want to tell him?" I asked.

She covered her chin with her palm. "It might be better if you did," she said. She drained her cup and got up from the table. "I'll get dressed."

Her bedroom door closed only moments before Angie and Dad arrived, carrying grocery bags.

"You'd better sit down," Toby said, cutting short their greetings. He wasn't going to let me waste time with small talk. They were still putting the bags on the counter when he put me on the spot. "Nora has some bad news." They sat, and looked at me expectantly.

"Dad," I said, reaching for his hand and holding it in both of mine. "I'm sorry to have to tell you this, but Uncle Bert is dead."

Dad drew back his hand. "What happened?"

Angie reached to put her hand on his shoulder, as if to keep him from collapsing forward. I gave him the facts quickly, watching as his face sank, blurring every feature that made him handsome. His blue eyes grew watery, his square jaw slacked, and his ivory skin turned gray. The transformation frightened me.

I searched for words and came out with, "I'm really sorry, Dad. I know that Uncle Bert wasn't always what he should have been, but—"

He lunged forward, slipping out of Angie's grip to grab at my arm. "Don't *you* start bad-mouthing him too," he growled. "Whatever he was, Bert was my brother."

"I'm sorry, Dad. I didn't mean it."

"Yes, you did," he said. "You and your mother never could stand him. You've made that very clear. Can't you see how much that hurts me? He's my brother. It's the same as if I insulted Angie. How would that make you feel?"

Angie recoiled into the back of her chair. She looked as frightened as I felt ashamed. Dad could insult his brother if he chose to—which he didn't. But Mom or I or Angie couldn't, according to some universal kinship rule. Angie had never transgressed that rule. Why had I? In desperation I said, "I don't know what I'm saying, Dad. Please forgive me."

His face reddened and he tucked his head on his chest. He started to cry, silently. Angie put her hand on the table in front of Dad and waited. He took her hand and held it as he composed himself. Then he asked, "Does Mom know?"

I nodded. "She's getting dressed."

Dad pushed himself back from the table and went to their room.

Toby sat down in Dad's place, and Angie refreshed the teapot. For the next quarter hour, Angie peppered me with questions and I replied mechanically. Toby listened but said nothing.

Murmurs from down the hall became louder, then softer, in waves. I looked toward the bedroom, hoping Mom and Dad would emerge united, ready to cope with the death in the family. But in order to help Dad mourn, Mom would have to alter her stance toward Bert, and I couldn't see that happening.

Mom came out of the bedroom alone, dressed now but looking even less composed than when she had left the kitchen. "Dad wants to see Bert's body. Can you arrange that?"

"But Mom," I objected. "The guards will arrive soon. We'd better all wait here. We can find out about seeing the body when they arrive."

She shot back, "Your father just lost his brother. He needs what he needs."

I apologized and left the room with as little fuss as possible. Mom had one thing right: it was Dad's tragedy. And she was clearly mad at me. What had I done? I had been insensitive with Dad. I wondered if our exchange had loosened Dad's resentment of how Mom had treated Bert. Had he lit into her, and did Mom think I had encouraged him to do so?

I walked out through the living room to the terrace, where lawn chairs beckoned. I needed a sit-down to calm myself and seek good sense. The strong sun of Midsummer Day was blocked by the house, which faced toward sunrise. The terrace in the back of the cottage faced west, overlooking a field that pitched for a mile, all the way to the sparkling ocean. At that moment, I felt like burrowing under a rock, but I settled into a lawn chair and tried not to think.

The door from the living room creaked, and I tensed. To my relief, it was Toby. He took the chair next to mine. He looked out at the sea for a long time and eventually closed his eyes. When I copied him, tears came. I let them wet my face. As quiet breathing returned, I opened my eyes, and Toby handed me a tissue. He always keeps one, folded into a small square, in his left-hand pocket. It's annoying when I find one shredded in the washing machine, but now it was much appreciated.

"I'm such a jerk," I said, patting at my cheeks. "I didn't mean to offend Dad. But what can I do? Bert's death is going to hurt him more than I would have thought. He wants me to act like I respected Uncle Bert, but that's not going to be easy. Mom knows how I feel." A choked laugh came out of me. "I feel just the way she taught me to feel."

"Your mother may be regretting that."

"Maybe she's regretting that I let Dad see it. She'll blame me for letting it show how we feel about him."

"Look, none of this is your fault. We've got more to deal with here than family dynamics. What about the button that you found? We didn't get very far pursuing it with your mother, did we?"

"No. I couldn't ask her point blank."

"Maybe you should try."

"Look, could you ask *your* mother point blank if she was a killer?"

"I guess not," Toby admitted.

It was a purely hypothetical question. Susan Sandler was a well-turned-out housewife from Mill Valley whose days were filled with tennis lessons, committee meetings, and charity work in Marin County. The only thing I could picture her murdering was a gin and tonic. In fact, I had often heard her make that avowal after a round of golf. How could I expect Toby to understand my relationship with my mother when we had been raised in such different circumstances? His cool and cultured parents rarely expressed their emotions and never raised their voices. Despite his upbringing, Toby was warmhearted and open. He tried to be sensitive to my needs. I was grateful for his even temperament, which was a Sandler family trait, but the tensions within my family eluded his grasp.

Suddenly I felt alone. No one, not even Toby, understood my dilemma. Only I had seen Bert's mangled body. Only I had found a sign that Mom had been at the scene of the crime. Only I had heard years of Mom's anger against him. Actually, she had given Dad an earful; but there were days when she talked with me endlessly, replaying scenes and analyzing Bert's psychology and Dad's in terms I don't think she would have shared with Dad. She wasn't exactly discreet with Angie and Eddie either, but for frank complaints against Bert the bastard, Mom had turned to me.

The crunch of tires on gravel announced the arrival of the detectives. We held back a few minutes before going in. By the time we crossed the living room to the kitchen, Detective Inspector O'Donnell and Sergeant Flynn were standing near the front door; so was Dad, as if barring their entry. Mom and Angie were seated at the table. Dad had been speaking, but he was interrupted by our arrival. I quickly introduced Toby to O'Donnell and Flynn. Dad, irritated with the men, continued: "So when *can* we see him, then? I have the right to see my brother's body."

O'Donnell discreetly eyed his mild-mannered colleague, who spoke gently to Dad. "I'm sorry, sir, but that won't be possible for a few days. He's been identified by his wife as well as by your daughter, and the body is now on the way to the morgue for autopsy."

"And where will that take place?" demanded Dad.

"At Mayo General Hospital in Castlebar. We'll notify you, sir, as soon as the body can be released."

Dad shook his head.

O'Donnell turned to me and spoke in a firmer tone. "Do you have your statement for me?"

I pulled it out of my pocket and gave it to him. Looking preoccupied, he handed it over to Flynn and turned back to Dad.

"We're aware this is a hard time for your family, but there are questions that must be asked." His eyes swept the small quarters. "It might be better if we did this at the station. Would you be willing to come with us, please? Just Mr. and Mrs. Barnes for now," he clarified, pointing to Mom and Dad. "It shouldn't take long."

"Where are we going?" asked Mom.

"To the garda station here on Achill," the inspector replied. "Just a few minutes away."

"Are we under arrest?" asked Mom, now agitated.

"Is there any reason you should be?" countered O'Donnell.

"Of course not!" she replied hotly.

"No one is under arrest," Sergeant Flynn said in a conciliatory tone. "Coming to the station is purely voluntary." At least for now, I told myself.

"Sergeant Flynn here will drive you," said the inspector.

"I'll get your coat," Dad said. In a moment, he was helping Mom into her raincoat, with the tenderness of a caress. They left the cottage silently.

It sounds like they'll be a while, then," Toby said. "I think Angie wants to talk to you alone." He gave Angie an encouraging look.

"You wouldn't mind?" asked Angie.

"Of course not. You two, talk." To me he said, "I haven't showered yet. I'll see you back at the cottage." I took his nod of the chin as encouragement to bare all to Angie.

She reached out to hug me. "You've been through the wringer," she said. (It was one of Grammy's sayings—Grammy was old enough to remember her grandmother putting washed clothes through the wringer before putting them out to dry.) Angie patted my shoulder before releasing me. "First you found the body, and then you had to break the news to Dad. I'm sorry it didn't go well." That's as close as Angie ever comes to reproach. She isn't blind to human error. She looks it in the face and feels nothing but dismay.

Angie is the "little sister" I treasure. She was born when I was twelve and my maternal hormones were newly released. It was just the right age to have a baby to hold. These days I try to treat her as my friend, my sister, not my "little" anything. She's six feet tall, gorgeous, funny, and full of love. She has a lot to teach me, even though I taught her the basics: riding a bicycle, baking a cake, getting on with Mom when she's in a mood. She now does all these things better than I ever did.

Angie has explored a world that I withdrew from as a teen, the world of the Catholic Church. She's religious enough to have entered a convent for a trial period, but she recently put off taking vows, much to the family's relief. I have a hard time picturing Angie as a nun. The list of her former boyfriends isn't short. At this moment, though, she had the bearing of a pensive saint, her eyes cast down and to the side.

"I'm worried about Mom and Dad," she said.

"Yes, this brings up all the old stuff about Uncle Bert." I decided to level with her. "It's the one conflict they've never resolved. You know Mom can't stand him. And she has good reason."

Glad to have Angie to confide in, I told her about the argument Mom had with Bert at the Jubilee, which she hadn't witnessed. I voiced my fear that Mom might come under suspicion once Aunt Laura talked to the police about the Jubilee dinner.

"Mom couldn't have had anything to do with Uncle Bert's death," Angie insisted. "We just got here yesterday. When do they think he died?"

"I don't know. They sent me away before the medical examiner had done his work. But it looked to me as if the blood was fairly set, as if it wasn't done this morning. Perhaps last night. If that's true, she's in the clear. Mom told me you all stayed in after dinner."

Angie went over to the sink to finish the dishes that Mom had abandoned when Toby and I arrived. "Give me a hand," she said. "I'll rinse and you put them in the dishwasher." We worked in silence till the job was done. As I passed her a towel to dry her hands on, she met my eyes. "I think I should tell you something. Mom went out last night when Dad and I were watching TV. She wanted to take a little walk. I'd already changed into my nightgown, so I didn't offer to go with her."

"She did say she stepped out for some air for a few minutes."

"It could have been longer."

That was not what I wanted to hear. Angie said that it was still dusk when Mom left, since it was Midsummer Eve, the longest day of the year. So they didn't worry about her being out. But I was plenty worried.

I asked, "Did you talk to her when she came back?"

"I was already in my bedroom, so I didn't see her come in. Dad had conked out. The drive from Galway did him in. He fell asleep after ten minutes in front of the TV. I had to wake him and send him off to bed. I told Dad I'd wait up for Mom, but I fell asleep too. At some point I woke and went to bed. I turned over when I heard Mom come in, but I didn't check the time. I just went back to sleep."

"Was it still dusk by then or dark?"

"There was still some light outside when I went to my room."

"But when you heard her come in?"

"I'm not sure. The curtains were closed."

"So it's conceivable she could have been gone for a short time just as she said, right?"

"Right," said Angie, looking relieved. "Right," she repeated to herself as she hung the dish towel back on its hook. Relief wasn't what I was feeling, though I saw no benefit in letting Angie worry. At my suggestion, she headed outside to unwind for a while by lounging on the terrace.

Meanwhile, I took the opportunity to slip into Mom and Dad's bedroom to find the sweater. Entering the cramped room, I looked around for Mom's clothes; nothing was lying out. I checked the closet; the sweater wasn't there. That left the bureaus. I went through all the drawers. No.

There was only one place left to look. I stepped into the bathroom and checked the towel hooks on the inside of the door. At home, Mom always hangs her clothes there. Sure enough, she had left the robe and apron she had been wearing in the kitchen. The robe was bunched out as if something was underneath it. I hesitated. I could turn and walk away and never know. Maybe that was the thing to do. No. I couldn't. I lifted the robe. Hanging underneath was Mom's blue cardigan.

And the buttons matched. I knew that at a glance, but just to make sure, I reached into my pocket and pulled out the one I had found next to Bert's body. There wasn't any doubt. It was silvery, polished, identical. My eye went to the spot where the sweater was missing a button. It would have been the third, positioned where a woman's bust tends to strain the wool. There was just a nub of thread remaining at that spot. For a moment, I thought of sewing the thing back on. Then sanity returned. What would Mom think when the missing button reappeared—that the fairies did it? What would Toby say? What would my conscience say? And what would the law say? That I was an accessory after the fact?

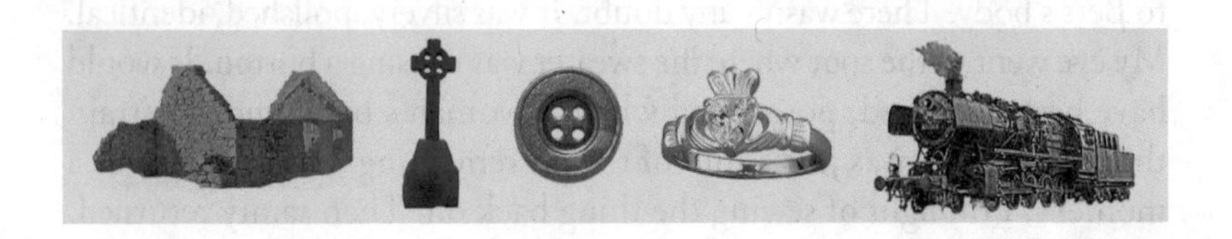

3

I WAS STANDING BY OUR BED, punching up the pillows.

"And you're sure the buttons match?"

"Yeah." My own leaden tone alarmed me.

"That still doesn't mean she's guilty, you know."

"Toby, this has got to be the worst day of my life." I socked one of the pillows hard, disgorging a few feathers.

"That's right. Give 'em a beating," Toby urged. "I'll join you." He feinted at the pillows on his side of the bed, and I had to laugh.

"Hop on," he ordered, and we plopped onto the saggy mattress. Toby pulled me to his side and flipped me so my head fell on his chest. I wanted to relax into his warm body, but parts of me stayed stiff. Understanding, Toby loosened his embrace and said, "Talk to me."

"That's the wife's line," I protested.

"I mean it. Tell me what you're thinking."

I did, and felt better when I had finished.

We went back to the other cottage soon after we heard the car bring my parents home and then depart. It was nearing suppertime, and Angie was heating up a prepared meal from the grocers. She said Mom and Dad were too tired to socialize. We should keep the meal short.

Socializing wasn't what I had in mind. I wanted to know what Mom had told the detectives. She reported that the interview room smelled of cigarettes and lye. Dad said he had been left in the lobby under the pitying gaze of the young female garda. I learned nothing during the family meal of chewy lamb patties and over-roasted potatoes.

In bed that night, nestled against Toby's bare skin, I confessed I was hurt that Mom hadn't shared anything with me. A wise inner voice said, *It's not about you*, so I corrected myself. "It can't be good that she's not talking. That means she's trapped. She feels she can't talk without revealing something."

"That could be anything," Toby said. "Maybe she's fighting with your father. You heard what he said about how your mother always bad-mouthed Bert. Now your dad's been robbed of his only brother. He's lost any chance to be closer to him. Could be he blames your mother." I drew back from Toby.

"No," he protested. "I don't mean he thinks she killed him. I mean she was always so angry with Bert that she kept your father from seeing him. And now he never will."

"That's not how it was, Toby. I'm sorry, you weren't there. She believed Bert was a crook and a liar. Of course she didn't want her kids exposed to him, but she never stopped Dad from seeing him." Toby propped himself up on an elbow and looked at me. I shut up and thought. Then I did a revision. "Okay, so she did keep our families apart."

We talked about what Bert had done. We talked about being judgmental. We talked about truth, speculation, and distortion, until I couldn't talk anymore. Toby rubbed my back and said my feelings were understandable. As I suspected, there was a "but." "But your feelings aren't the facts. The facts will come out, and when they do, whatever they are, we'll face them."

I woke to the ping of a text. As I suspected, it was Angie. "Come to u at 10. See Laura Emily 10:30." I tapped my question: "Who sees them?" Instant reply: "You and me. Condolence call." Apparently, she had committed me, so I texted back: "ok." I left Toby smiling in his sleep. (I always wonder what that's about.)

The walk to Aunt Laura's retraced the route I had taken the morning before, since Uncle Bert's house lay just beyond the Deserted Village. It was a warm morning, with a pleasant breeze rippling through the roadside shrubbery. I let the swing of my arms relieve my tension, while Angie recounted the drama of the previous night.

She told me that after dinner Dad decided to visit Aunt Laura and asked Mom to go with him, but she refused. He created a lot of noise leaving the house, and he made the car wheels spin in the gravel. Mom went into her bedroom. Angie respected the closed door and stayed in the kitchen, doing the dishes. When Dad returned, he told Angie that Laura looked broken. That didn't surprise him; Bert had been her whole life. It worried him more that Emily was silent, closed in upon herself. That's what gave him the idea that Angie and I should visit in the morning. Emily needed someone her own age to talk to, he said.

It must have been hard for Dad to face Aunt Laura. He knew she had told the detectives about the argument between Mom and Bert at the Jubilee dinner, because the inspector's questions had started there. In spite of that, he knew his duty. He visited his brother's widow, but he was unable to provide comfort. Angie felt that Dad wanted us to succeed where he had failed—a tall order, in my opinion. Aunt Laura couldn't be expected to have warm feelings toward anyone in our family. But maybe Dad was right and we could console our cousin.

We rounded a bend in the road and Angie got her first glimpse of the Deserted Village, where I had found Bert's body. Even from this distance the little town looked spooky, with its hundred abandoned houses clinging to the slope of Slievemore Mountain. Looking at the ruins from afar, I thought of the writer Heinrich Böll, who came to Achill after World War II, seeking refuge from the horrors he had witnessed as a soldier drafted into the German army. He wrote a memoir about his time on the island called *Irish Journal*, which I had read before the trip. He was fascinated by the Deserted Village, where instead of the detritus of bombed-out cities, he found only crumbling walls and chimneys, the elements having slowly eaten away thatched roofs, wooden doors, and everything else but stone. He was struck by the thought that this was what a village looked like if left to die a natural death, instead of being destroyed by war.

But with Bert's death the village had become the scene of a violent crime. Pointing up the hill to the tent with a single figure standing at the entry flap, Angie asked, "Is that where you found the body?" She wanted a recap, step by step. I took her through it again as we turned our back on the village, heading straight toward the sea.

According to Dad's directions, Bert's house would be found on a side lane opposite a farmhouse and a meadow spotted with sheep. The farmhouse came into view just as I caught the faint line of the ocean in the distance. The entrance to the lane wasn't visible yet, obscured by bushes, but I could see the house on the bare hill above. Too substantial to be called a cottage, Bert's rental property fit its location well. Its footprint was small, but the house rose high, to three stories. From the top floors, you would be able to spot boats sailing in the bay at Keel or passing by the treacherous Minaun Cliffs. From the other side of the house you would have a view of Slievemore Mountain and the whole Deserted Village. And on the sides between, you would be looking at the sunrise or sunset. Leave it to Bert to snag the best location on the island.

I mentally slapped my wrist for harboring that resentful thought. We were here to offer comfort, I reminded myself. But truth to tell, I had another agenda for the visit. I wanted to find out what Aunt Laura was thinking. Did she know anything that might throw light on the murder and help put my mother in the clear? For instance, when did Bert leave the house? Was that the last time she saw him? What was he doing at the Deserted Village? Did she know of anyone who had a motive to attack him?

Emily opened the door before we knocked. Thin, blond, and fine-featured, she looked fragile enough to break under stress. As a child, I had envied her delicate beauty. I used to think of her as the angel on the top of the Christmas tree: radiant, otherworldly, and too far above me to touch. We grew up and I stopped believing in angels, but I never felt at ease with my cousin. Thrown together occasionally at holidays, we found things to do—we would play cards or she would tell stories—but she seemed to live on another plane. Now it was her grief that set her apart from us. She gave us a whispered welcome and took us to the living room. Aunt Laura was standing erect, awaiting our arrival. In spite of her upright posture, she seemed about to fold like a marionette.

"Mama, sit down," Emily said in a low voice. "You're supposed to be resting."

My aunt stepped forward and opened her arms to me. It was the first time we had embraced since I was a child, and it felt artificial. There was absolutely no cushion on Laura's bones. She was meanly thin, and she held herself stiff. It was like hugging a skeleton. She touched her cheek to mine and then turned to greet Angie.

"We're so sorry about Uncle Bert," said Angie.

Laura nodded in acknowledgment and let Angie hug her.

I said I was sorry too and that Dad was heartbroken.

"Yes, I could tell he was when he came to see us, dear." Her scratchy voice suggested real concern.

"Dad always spoke well of Uncle Bert," I said. "He loved him."

"I believe he did." She looked at me with sorrow in her eyes. Who knows what she was thinking, perhaps that her husband was hurt by Dad's coolness, or perhaps that she knew what had kept them apart. Then again, Aunt Laura's eyes were always sad. Despite her perfect makeup and fashion-model's figure, her eyes betrayed her age or, rather, her suffering, whatever it was.

She sat down on the couch and gestured for me to join her. Angie took a chair, and Emily went into the kitchen to make tea. Angie and I probably should have opened a conversation, but neither of us did. Finally Laura said, "They told me you were the one who found him." She leaned toward me, her body sending an appeal for a moment of shared anguish. But a lifetime of aversion had raised a barrier on my side that death couldn't lower.

"It was ghastly," I replied, too bluntly. "I was walking in the Deserted Village and I found him stretched out on the ground. It's horrible to think he might have been lying there all night. Do the guards think that's what happened?"

"Yes, they put the time of death at between 8:00 p.m. and midnight." Her voice caught, but she continued. "He went out to the ruins after dinner. Bert often goes there in the evening. You know, we've been here on and off since the spring because of his work." She said "because of his work" with reverence, as if the world had just lost a man of great achievements. "His main project is over near the causeway, but he also wanted to restore part of the Deserted Village. That's why he rented here, to have it nearby and in his thoughts. He liked to walk there and think about how it could be done."

"I see. When did you start to worry?"

"I didn't know anything was wrong. He usually comes to bed after I do. But he wasn't there in the morning." Her scrawny hands went to her mouth.

"Is that when you called the guards?" I asked.

"I didn't call them. I thought Bert came in late and then went out early. The guards came to the house, after he was found." Her face contorted, and she covered it with her hands. We waited until she regained control.

Angie responded. "It must have been a shock, hearing that from the police. I'm sorry. Nora broke the news to my parents. Then some detectives showed up at our place and took them in for questioning. Dad says the detectives were hard on Mom. I hope they were kinder with you."

Laura folded her hands in her lap, like a pupil in grade school. "I suppose. They didn't give me time to take it in. They asked me so many questions, so fast."

"I understand you told them about the argument Mom had with Uncle Bert at the Jubilee." I tried to keep my tone neutral.

Laura looked up. "Well, you know, I had to. They asked about things like that." She sounded defensive but forthright.

"You don't really think our mom had anything to do with what happened to Uncle Bert, do you?" asked Angie.

Laura looked at her fingers, knotted tightly in her lap. "Surely not," she said. It could have been more forceful.

"Because she didn't," said Angie.

Laura's lips tightened into a line. We sat in a frozen tableau until Emily returned with the tea. She set the tray on a table, to allow the tea to steep.

"We've been over all this with the guards," Laura said.

I apologized. "You're right. This isn't the time or place. It's just that they've been questioning us too and I'm trying to get the facts straight. It's been upsetting for Mom and Dad."

Angie added, "It's a bad time for everyone in the family." She was right. Grief was the appropriate topic now, not guilt or suspicion.

"I'm sorry if I sounded insensitive," I said. "How can we help right now? Is there anything we can do for you, either of you?"

"It's kind of you to ask," said Laura. "We'll be all right, won't we, dear?"

"Yes," said Emily. She roused herself to check whether the tea was ready. It wasn't.

"Do you have everything you need in the house? Do you need anything from the store?" asked Angie, addressing Emily.

"No. Nothing," said Emily. She checked the tea again.

While she was pouring, the front door opened and a man burst in. It occurred to me only later that he hadn't knocked. He was stocky but good-looking, in a very Irish way—bluebell eyes, peaches-and-cream complexion, thick white hair, and handsome bone structure. He reminded me of Ted Kennedy in his middle years. "Laura—" he began, but he stopped when he saw that she had company. "I'm sorry, I didn't know . . ."

"It's fine, Frank," she assured him. "These are my nieces, Nora and Angie. They're the daughters of Bert's brother." We stood and shook hands.

"I'm Frank Hickey," he said. "Bert's partner. And friend," he added. "It's a shame we have to meet under these circumstances."

"Frank was born and raised on Achill," Laura said. "He knows every hill, beach, and bog. Bert relied on him."

She gestured for us all to sit. Frank thanked Emily for the cup she handed him, but he placed it on a side table without taking a sip and went on, still in a hurry. "I'm just after talking to the guards," he said. "I told them I was worried something like this could happen, what with the sniping we've had. I gave them names too. I want you to know we'll find out who did this."

Aunt Laura said by way of explanation, "Frank and Bert have been having words with some of the locals who are against their plans."

Frank shook his head in dismay. "I said it was only a matter of time till there was violence."

"Is this about the restoration of the Deserted Village?" I asked.

"Partly," said Frank. He cleared his throat, as if it was hard for him to talk about this. "Bert had a grand design," he said, raising one hand dramatically. "He had vision, your uncle. He could see that Achill was ripe for development and we could bring in double or triple the number of tourists with the right combination of attractions. For starters, we're building a boutique hotel at the entrance to the causeway, where the old railroad station used to be. There'll be no place as posh in all of County Mayo. Then Bert thought of turning the Deserted Village into an outdoor museum with some of the cottages restored to the way they were. We'll hire local people as guides to demonstrate the old ways of life and that sort of thing."

I could picture it already: a theme park with women in period dress showing tourists how to spin wool and hawking souvenirs and chocolate bars. No wonder there was opposition to it.

"His grandest plan," Frank continued, "was to bring back a section of the railway that used to run between Westport and Achill. They closed the line in the thirties. Then they tore up the tracks and made the railbed into a greenway for hiking and biking. Mind you, we'd only use a sliver of it for a new stretch of track. We'd bring in an old steam locomotive and a passenger car for a ride from Westport right up to the hotel. Families with kids love that sort of thing. It'd bring visitors to the island and be good for economic growth. And there'd still be plenty of space left for the bike path. But we've got a bunch of angry environmentalists trying to block the project. There've been protests and smutty letters and even threats. It's ended in this."

I sat up straighter in my chair. "Are you saying someone who was against the project killed my uncle?"

"It's a good bet," said Frank. "People on the island are fuming about the rail project."

"Is there anyone in particular you suspect?" I asked. The surest way to clear Mom of suspicion would be to identify the real assailant.

"I'll not mention names here. But you can be sure I gave the guards plenty of leads." He reached over and squeezed Laura's hand. She held on with the grip of a drowning woman.

"What will happen to your plans now?" asked Angie.

"It's not up to me alone," Frank answered. "Others are involved. We formed a syndicate. I've a feeling they'll want to push ahead. In fact, I'm on my way now to a meeting to discuss it." He stood up, with Laura still gripping his hand. "Laura, I just stopped by to tell you I've been to the guards. I have to go now." He lowered his voice. "I'm sorry for your trouble. Truly I am."

They looked into each other's eyes, until he broke away. I had the impression he wanted to stay longer and would have done so if Angie and I had not been there.

"I'm glad to know you," he said to us, "in spite of the occasion."

"We should get back too," I said to Laura and Emily. "Again, if there's anything you need . . ."

"Thank you," said Laura. I felt we hadn't been much comfort to them, after all. We exchanged another round of awkward hugs and moved to follow Frank out.

"Don't worry. We're okay," said Emily. She turned away before we reached the door. She had certainly changed since our youth. Maybe it was maturity, or maybe it was grief. Her skin, once creamy, looked as thin as skim milk. Her movements, once expansive, were now stiff and awkward. Her clipped sentences were nothing like the lively monologues I remembered. She seemed diminished.

4

WALKING OUT INTO THE MOIST ISLAND AIR, I considered what we had heard about opposition to Bert's development plans. Frank Hickey had pointed the guards in that direction. Maybe Mom had nothing to do with Bert's death, but it didn't resolve my dilemma about her lost button. I was still holding it back.

Angie's voice cut through my brooding. "Wasn't that supposed to be a condolence call? I don't think we were very consoling." I couldn't disagree.

By way of distraction, we made a game of trying to identify plants by the side of the road. Ferns abounded, but we didn't know the types. The rosy purple bells bunched on stalks looked like the lupine in marsh-land back home; they were profuse along the ditch at the verge. When we came to the farm at the end of the lane, there were masses of calla lilies. The farmer's wife must have planted those, I thought. But the farm didn't look as if a wife lived there. A woman wouldn't let an old tractor rust in the side yard next to a muddied hatchback. And though it was picturesque to see a rooster strutting around the tractor while his harem picked at the grass, the hens were a little too close to the road for safety.

The meadows around the house stretched far back, so far that no other houses were in view. In the distance, grazing sheep seemed planted in the grass like daisies, sometimes singly, sometimes in clumps. Angie slowed up, assessed the site, and said, "You know, this is just the kind of place I'd like to live in. Life would be simple—your garden, your animals, and a view of the ocean or the mountain any time you wanted to look. It feels like God's in his heaven and all's right with the world." (All's right? Only if you don't think about it. Bert's death, family strife, our mother under suspicion of murder. There's no getting around the problem of evil.) Instead of saying anything, I smiled. I protect my sisterly bond with Angie by keeping such thoughts to myself.

Angie gave the place a longing glance, and we turned to face Slievemore Mountain. The soft green of summer grass blended with the gray of the ruins clinging to the slope, but the noonday sun caught a patch of stark white. That would be the evidence tent over the ruin where I had found Bert. I also noticed a van in the parking lot below. White, with yellow stripes. "Looks like the only people visiting the village are official," I said. "The guards must have closed it to tourists." I wondered if the technical team had found any useful evidence.

"Oh, rats," Angie complained. "I wanted to see it up close. Let's at least go read those panels." She pointed at information boards across the parking lot, next to the gate to the village. The first one offered nothing but rules and regulations. The other gave a history of the site. It mentioned megalithic tombs but didn't disclose where they were. It attested to settlement from the Middle Ages till the Great Famine that began in 1845, when villagers abandoned the site and moved closer to the sea, a sure source of food. From that time, families sent their sheep and cattle to the mountain in summer, accompanied by youngsters who would spend the day tending them. The shepherds would use a ruin as a day-house and would carry milk down the mountain to the family at evening. I wondered what they did on a rainy day, with no roof overhead. Maybe they made a tent like the one over the crime scene.

The blast of a horn made me jump. Someone was driving up the dirt road fast, honking like a seal. The car halted ten yards beyond us, and a spotted black-and-white dog sprang out. It ran at full speed up the hillside, on a mission to corral a flock of sheep that was grazing below the line of ruins. Sharp whistles came from inside the car. A tall man jumped out, whistling and calling. The message to the dog was clear: Get those sheep out of where they don't belong. The dog barked roughly and darted back and forth, frightening the sheep up the hill, forcing them into a run toward the crumbling walls of the village. Most of the flock headed where they had been sent, but the dog kept running to confront outliers, pushing them up the hill.

When the sheep were assembled in a single group, the man knew that his dog needed no more signals to get the job done. Waving cheerfully to us, he called, "Hi! How are ya?" and apologized for the ruckus. He explained that his sheep belonged farther up, on the steeps. During the night they had drifted all the way down to the road. No one complained until four sheep wandered into the graveyard below the west end of the village. Then he got a phone call from the lady who keeps a guesthouse in the old presbytery. "Good thing she didn't call the guards," the man said, nodding toward the white van. "They're trouble and strife."

He introduced himself as Bobby Colman, owner of a VW Golf and one very smart dog. "Blackie, there, she's a class herder." He pointed toward an invisible presence up the hill. I could tell already that Bobby was a talker, and he didn't disappoint. Angie asked if he called himself a shepherd. "Blackie's the shepherd," he laughed. "I'm the fella that feeds Blackie. She runs the flock from field to pasture. Then she rounds them up when they stray. Once in a while she chases them back to the farm, to be sheltered, or sheared, or what have you. I'm just her drudge." He winked at Angie and gave me a crooked smile.

Hmm, I thought. He's the flirter. Angie's the flirtee. And I'm the duenna who needs to be won over. Bobby was easy to look at, probably closer to my age than Angie's. His flat-weave fisherman's sweater, gray with wear, stretched tightly over wide shoulders and a full chest. Snug jeans, tucked into muck boots, revealed a slim lower half. Back home I would have taken him for a swimmer or a quarterback, but it was hard farming that gave Bobby his barrel chest. While his body looked strong and controlled, his face was free, expansive with laughter. I noticed Angie noticing, as well as Bobby noticing that Angie was noticing.

He charmed us for more than an hour, long enough for me to have to sidle over to the gate for something to lean against. With Angie's encouragement, Bobby the Shepherd gave us his life story, and more. He had been kicked out of school for being too wild, he confessed, and he was glad of it. "Those uni types are soft," he declared. "No confidence. Confidence comes from hard work and discipline." He learned that from his first big job, in England, as foreman at a Goodyear plant. "I'd take one of our young Irish bucks for ten of their city lads. Weaklings, they were. Yell at 'em once, and they quit the job." He was glad to return to Achill after eight years, with pounds in his pocket. His parents gave him the homecoming of the prodigal son.

"I'm one of many," he said. "We left when there was no work here, returned when there was no work there. All my old pals came home—from Canada, the States, Australia, England. They brought families back too, every one of 'em. I should have done the same, but now I'm an Irish bachelor taking care of me old dear and five hundred fat sheep."

"Five hundred? That's amazing!" Angie's big blue eyes said the same.

I asked, "Are all five hundred up the mountain? That's a lot of sheep for Blackie to herd."

Bobby smiled at our ignorance. "I don't send more than a hundred to one spot. Don't want to overgraze the common land, nor my own neither. I've got four meadows just over there." He nodded toward the farm we had passed, the one Angie had admired. I could see it coming. Angie lit up with pleasure and, in the most innocent way, flattered the man silly with praises of his home. What could I do but let the scene play out?

This wasn't the first time I had watched Angie fall for a guy and the guy fall for her, even if he was totally inappropriate. Last year it was a French gendarme who didn't mention he was engaged. The one before that was a barista with plans to better himself by stealing motorcycles.

There were a few others too. Lovely, naïve Angie had a history of falling into the arms of the wrong man. The family was dubious when, after the barista breakup, she announced she was entering a convent. We had a feeling that this spiritual romance would prove as short-lived as her more earthly ones. Instead, she was more faithful to Grace Quarry than any of her lovers had been to her. She kept the promises of a "sojourner" for a full year and then had a slip right under the nose of her mother superior, who, in the spirit of infinite mercy, took her back. Angie spent the next year working in a shelter for battered women. At the end of that term, she decided to put off taking final vows. I had feared that seeing the sufferings of women abused by men would solidify Angie's choice of the celibate life, but instead, it seemed, the job forced Angie to face hard realities. She began to suspect what everyone else already knew: she did not, after all, "have a vocation" as a nun. For Angie, this trip to Ireland was a strategic break from the convent, a time to consider re-entering the world.

"The sheep are just my day job, you know," Bobby went on. "I have a band too, the best on the island. You should come hear us. We're playing tonight."

"Really?" Angie said. "What's your instrument?"

"The fiddle. The banjo too. And I sing. We'll be at the Annexe, just over in Keel." He gestured toward the sea. "Why don't you come?"

"What time do you play?" asked Angie.

"The usual. We start at nine and go until closing. You should both come." He looked my way, making a conscious gesture to include me. I thanked him for the invitation and, just to be polite, I said we would try to make it.

"Super!" said Angie. "We'll be there."

5

OUR COTTAGE WAS EMPTY when I got back. I welcomed the solitude and crept into bed. As soon as I stretched out, I felt myself sliding into a heavy sleep, the kind that comes from emotional weight.

I was deep into a thought-obliterating snooze when the sound of a strumming harp jerked me up fast. On one elbow, I located my phone and answered the call, feeling invaded and cranky. It was my one friend in Ireland, Maggie McBride, an art historian from Dublin. We had met the previous winter at a conference in France and managed to stay close through emails, texts, and FaceTime. Maggie was fun, and Toby was fond of her too, so we had asked her to meet us while we were on Achill. She accepted, on her own terms: namely, she would find her own lodging, and she couldn't say just when she would come. This call announced her arrival. She was at a teahouse nearby and could be with us in minutes—bearing chocolate cake and her dog, Happy.

A visit from Maggie was just what I needed. It didn't take long for us to get sloppy with cake and frosting. Pretty quickly I got sloppy with emotions too. Somehow, my redheaded, cheerful friend drew all my feelings to the surface. She got to see the strain I had been hiding from my parents and listened patiently to my story, edited to exclude the button. After a while, I composed myself and we looked at my uncle's death from every angle, although I didn't share my deepest fear about Mom. Then Maggie slapped her hand on the table. Happy barked assent. He had been a frisky puppy when I had last seen him. He was almost fully grown now but just as rambunctious and affectionate.

"We're going out," Maggie announced. "You need to clear your head." What Maggie had in mind was the Atlantic Drive, a touristic circuit of rural roads leading to miles of seaside cliffs. It would be my first chance to see the rest of the island, and I leapt at the idea. I hoped that Toby and my parents were doing the same, not wasting a fine day at the garda station.

While driving swiftly, way too swiftly, past bogs and scruff, Maggie brought me up to date on her love life. Toby and I had met her at a conference in France at the beginning of her romance with a graduate student named Thierry, who was younger than Maggie by more than a decade. We liked him very much. Maggie's dalliance with Thierry (pronounced tee-ary) had blossomed into a love affair, which lasted the six months of Maggie's research leave in France. It would be put to the test this fall, with Maggie back teaching in Dublin. She was frank about the challenge of maintaining a long-distance relationship but didn't sound deeply concerned. I was concerned for Thierry, however, when I learned where she was staying on Achill.

"My friend Declan has a cottage on Keel strand. He's putting me up."

"Is he one of your exes?" I asked. Maggie, I knew, had gone through a number of "friends" before Thierry. She referred to them in the plural as her exes.

"He is, and we've stayed in touch. You'll meet him. He owns a gallery in Dublin specializing in Irish paintings. He collects for himself as well." Maggie's description of the collection intrigued me, and I was equally intrigued by the warmth in her voice when she spoke of her ex. It led me to wonder if he was really exed-out or if he was more an ex-plus.

A sharp turn off the main road put us on a narrow, gently curving road lined with pink rhododendrons. Beyond the bright bushes lay bare flatlands massed with yellow gorse. For a stretch, land that had been harvested long ago was now a bog. The black turf, cut into trenches and boxes, was blanketed by mauve grass. Soon the bog gave way to sandy flats, and suddenly at our left lay the waters of Achill Sound, gray and unruffled. A passing cloud had put land and sea in shadow. It was in that moody light that I first saw the ruin of Kildownet Church.

Maggie tilted her head toward the church, acknowledging the presence of a site worth exploring. She slowed as we approached an acre of ancient tombstones, both small and grand. We pulled to the side, well before the church, and Maggie let Happy out. "My boy needs a run," she said. "Walk around and get the feel of the place. Then I'll tell you about it." She took off after Happy, who was dodging standing crosses as he ran toward the water.

I felt myself drawn to the old church. The roof was completely gone, but the stonework stood firm. Someone had strewn pebbles over the floor of the nave. At the east end, right where it belonged, stood an altar constructed of a four-foot base stone topped by a slab the size of a coffee table. The structure looked new, perhaps only a guess at what stood for an altar eight hundred years ago. Visitors had treated it like a tomb, placing rocks on the tabletop in tribute to the dead.

Outside, I roamed among plots studded with blunt stone crosses buried up to their arms, a section behind the church with slabs flat on the ground, and a graveled terrace close to the sea. I heard Happy scampering and saw Maggie coming. She told me I was treading on the Famine grave, filled with the bones of starved men, women, and children. "The anonymity of all these dead is humbling, isn't it?" she said. "In the other field, you see headstones you can read. They're trying to fight oblivion with a stone and a name. Can't be done for this poor lot."

That led my thoughts back to my uncle. Burial in a cemetery back home would include a gravestone giving him the dignity of a name, but only a successful investigation would establish responsibility for his death.

"Of course it's the communal graves connected with the prophecy that everyone comes to see," Maggie went on.

"What prophecy?" I asked.

"Do you not know about the Achill prophecy?"

"I guess not."

"Folks swear it's true. Now, some of them believe in leprechauns." She smiled.

"Even so, let me hear it," I said. We stood side by side, looking out across Achill Sound, as Maggie told the story.

"It goes back to the seventeenth century, when an Irish prophet named Brian the Red predicted that, one day, carriages on iron wheels would come to Achill Island, belching smoke and fire. What's more, on their first and final journeys, these carriages would be carrying the dead. Sure enough, when the railroad came to Achill in the 1890s, the first train carried home the bodies of thirty migrants who had drowned on their way to jobs across the sea in Scotland."

"How awful," I said.

"That was just the first tragedy," continued Maggie. "In the thirties, a score of boys from Achill, also migrant laborers in Scotland, died in a terrible fire. Their bodies also came home by train, on the last run before the line shut down. They're buried over there." She pointed.

I followed Maggie into a plot of grass marked off by an iron fence topped with sharp iron crosses. At the far side of the enclosure stood a high tombstone listing the names of those drowned in 1894. There were as many women as men, and some Achill families lost more than one member. "You can see why the story became a legend," Maggie said. "The deaths were a calamity for the whole island."

"It's heartbreaking," I said. "I can see why people would resent my uncle's plan. A honky-tonk version of the railroad would mock the tragedies."

Maggie nodded. "Achill's a small island with a tiny population. There's hardly a family here that wasn't touched by one disaster or the other. The resentment could go deep."

Here was another possible motive for my uncle's murder and another avenue for the gardai to pursue.

Maggie consulted her watch. "Let's move on. I'd like to get out to the other end of the island and show you Keem Bay." She whistled for Happy, who came bounding out from behind a tombstone, his pink tongue lolling on one side of his mouth. He danced around Maggie's ankles as we walked to the car. "In you go," she said.

A short way beyond the graveyard, we passed a fifteenth-century watchtower that once belonged to the pirate queen Grace O'Malley. "She was a terror, that one," said Maggie. "My kind of woman."

The scenery grew flat again as we followed the perimeter of the island, with dramatic ocean views on one side of the road and windswept, treeless bogs on the other. Occasionally we passed whitewashed houses and Blackface mountain sheep. "Sheep outnumber people five to one on Achill," Maggie said, braking to allow a poky pair to meander across the road. We waited for the sheep to get across, and then we set out again. In the distance, green hills and gray mountains gave definition to the landscape. We also passed walls of imposing cliffs. Those at the western end of the island are said to be the tallest in Europe.

We turned inland near the hamlet of Dooega in order to join the main road leading out to Achill Head. This road spans the width of the island (about fifteen miles) from the Michael Davitt Bridge, linking the island to the mainland, all the way to the tip at Keem Bay. It passes through the tiny villages of Keel and Dooagh, the houses all white with gray tile roofs.

Then comes a spectacular stretch where the narrow road climbs steeply and the land falls away in a dizzying drop to the sea. I was glad I wasn't driving. For an American, it's bad enough to always be on the "wrong" side of the road in Ireland; here you are on the wrong side of the road at the edge of a cliff. "Almost there," said Maggie, by way of comfort. That was before a series of corkscrew turns.

Finally, she pulled into a dirt parking area looking out at ocean, cliffs, and, far below, a crescent, sandy beach. We got out to explore. The beach was pristine and deserted. Intrepid swimmers had access by means of a steep descending road, but there were no takers today. The water glowed with a surreal aquamarine light. "This used to be a favorite spot for shark fishing," said Maggie. Maybe that explained the absence of swimmers.

Happy bellied up to the edge to look over, his snout on his forelegs. We gazed for a minute or two. "Maggie," I said, breaking the spell, "what's the story with you and this guy you're staying with, if you don't mind my being nosy."

"Declan? We're just old friends. We used to be more, but that was years ago."

"So this is just a platonic visit?"

"More or less," said Maggie, wiggling one hand.

"Okay, then. What's he like?"

"Declan's older. A confirmed bachelor, lives by himself. He's well off and does what he pleases. He can be charming when he wants to. You can tell me if you think he's good-looking. He's smart. He thinks a lot of himself, though, and he's got a know-it-all side that puts some people off. We had fun for a while, but he was too pushy for me. Or maybe I wasn't ready for someone like that. I was young at the time."

"How do you mean, pushy?"

She looked at me slyly. "He wanted us to try a swingers' club! I was mortified, really I was. If I'd had time to consider, I might have come round, but Declan pushed me, and I didn't like it. I walked right out the door—didn't talk to him for five years."

I felt my eyebrows go up.

"I was a young eejit. I'd do differently now." She bent down to pull Happy back and lift him into her arms.

"You think you'd go?" I asked.

"Don't pretend to be surprised, girl. It's the twenty-first century."

"I'm not naïve," I protested. "I've heard of those clubs. Where was this, in Dublin?"

"They have them in Dublin for sure, but no. It was right here on the island."

"There was a swingers' club on Achill Island?"

"Not just 'was.' There still is. It's an open secret, and it's been going on for years. You know, there's not much else to do here, especially in the winter. The weather is miserable. There's nothing like a pagan orgy to warm things up. A small circle of locals keeps the thing going. At least, that's what Declan tells me."

I had a hard time getting my head around the idea. We had come to Achill on the advice of a nun, my cousin, to get a glimpse of the old ways of life in Ireland, expecting—what? Turf smoldering in the fireplace, Céillí dancers, fiddles and shillelaghs, tales about the little people, maybe, but certainly not this. "I'm speechless," I said (illogically). Wait until Toby hears about this, I thought.

6

"HERE ON THE ISLAND?" Toby exclaimed.

"Yup. That's what she said."

"You don't suppose we could—"

"No, I don't." I had enough on my mind with my uncle's murder and worrying about my mother's involvement. I didn't need the distraction of a sex club, even as a topic of conversation. My move to table the motion was abetted by the fact that we were out in public, but I knew that wouldn't be the end of it. "Just drink your Guinness," I counseled, pointing to the pint glass of black liquid crested by a thick layer of cream-colored foam. Toby shrugged and stared into his beer, daydreaming no doubt.

I was nursing a half pint of the bitter stuff myself but with a dollop of syrup swirled in to cut the aftertaste, strictly a ladies' drink in Ireland. "Guinness is good for you," they say. They do; signs all over Ireland say just that. It must be one of the most successful ad campaigns ever dreamed up. As I looked around the crowded pub, almost everyone had a glass of the dark brew in hand.

The musicians too had pints in front of them. When they weren't playing, they were sipping. Angie sat up close to the players, to get the full benefit of Bobby Colman's sexy baritone and flirtatious glances. There were three men in the band and six instruments among them. Bobby played the fiddle and a banjo, not at the same time. A huge, shaggy, copper-headed guy with an inflated chest and a bushy beard swapped between a tin whistle and a bagpipe. And a hunched-over elder kept time on the bodhran, a handheld drum resembling a tambourine. Now and again, he would switch to squeezing a small accordion. They played with raucous spirit, Bobby singing lead and the others joining on the chorus, with a combination of sentiment and defiance that only an Irish folk tune can evoke. The subject of this one was a young patriot named Roddy McCorley, who was hanged by the British during the 1798 rebellion. The pub was crowded; there was foot-stamping in the audience. "Up the rebels!" shouted a patron, and the cry was echoed by other men. Bobby Colman leaned forward and sang:

> Up the narrow street he stepped, so smiling, proud, and young,
> About the hemp rope on his neck, the golden ringlets clung;
> There's ne'er a tear in his blue eyes, fearless and brave are they,
> For young Roddy McCorley goes to die on the bridge of Toome today.

I was ready to grab a pitchfork and march to the bridge myself, to stop the execution.

"They're good," acknowledged Toby. "You can't beat the Irish for folk songs about martyrdom. It's something in the national character. When you keep losing battles and you've got a harp as the official emblem of your country, it's inevitable." He took a swig and wiped the foam from his lips. "It's the same with literature. Look how many of their writers have won the Nobel Prize—Yeats, Shaw, Beckett, Seamus Heaney. Joyce should have won but didn't. For such a little country, that's amazing."

"Why do you think that is?" I asked.

"I had a lit professor who thought it was because the Irish were held down so long by the British. Because their national aspirations were suppressed, they channeled their political passion into stories and music. I think there's something to it. There are probably more storytellers per acre in Ireland than anywhere else in the world."

"That's a clever theory you have there, Yank," said a voice behind us. The tables in the pub were pushed close together to accommodate the crowd, and our conversation had been overheard.

"It's meant as a compliment," said Toby, turning to glance behind him.

"So taken," said the man, reaching to pat Toby's shoulder, but his hand withdrew as he recognized me. I took a few seconds to register who he was. Then I realized it was up to me to make introductions. "Toby, this is Frank Hickey. We met at Aunt Laura's house. Mr. Hickey was Uncle Bert's business partner. This is my husband, Toby Sandler."

"It's Frank," he said, reaching over to shake Toby's hand. "Again, I'm sorry for your trouble," he said without meeting my eyes. "A terrible thing about your uncle." There was a silence, magnified by the absence of music. The band was on break. I noticed that Bobby Colman had drawn a chair up to Angie's table; he was elbow to elbow with her.

"Would you like to join us?" I asked. Frank seemed to be alone.

"Thanks, I will. I just stopped in to hear the boys," he said, as if his presence required an excuse. "Can I get you another pint?" he asked Toby, whose glass was half-empty. Mine he could see was still nearly full.

"Not yet," Toby said with a smile. "But thanks. It takes me a while to get through one of these."

"A big fella like you?" Frank scoffed. "Is it the black stuff you're drinking?"

Toby nodded, and Frank went up to the bar to order. While he was standing there waiting for the foamy heads to subside so the bartender could top off the pints, I filled Toby in on what I knew about Frank's connection to my uncle.

When he returned with the beers, Frank picked up the thread of his earlier remark. "You seem to know a good deal about Irish culture."

"Not really," said Toby. "I took a course in college on the Irish Literary Revival, so anything I picked up is secondhand and probably outdated."

"And are you a professor yourself?" Frank asked.

Toby put up a hand in denial. "Not me. I run an antiques gallery back home."

"Antiques, is it? Well, now. It's just that we see a lot of professors from the States here in the summer visiting Yeats's grave and such. And Laura tells me your wife is a university professor." He looked at me.

"Yes, I teach art history," I said.

"Ah," he said. "I wonder what your opinion is of our Irish painters. Do you have a favorite?"

Maggie would be the right person to answer that question, but she was at her ex's cottage tonight. My field is nineteenth-century European painting, mainly French. I would guess that anyone with a passing interest in art could name a French Impressionist, but how many could name an Irish painter of any type? Ireland's artists aren't as well known as her writers.

Of those I know, my favorite is Paul Henry, celebrated for his depictions of the Irish countryside. He was influenced by the Post-Impressionists, and he lived on Achill for a decade. I had brushed up on his work before the trip.

My answer seemed to please Frank. He clapped his hands and said, "Well, isn't that lovely. I'm proud to say I have a painting by Henry, or a share in it. Your uncle paid a lot of money for it at a Dublin auction. It was for the business; even so, if you ask me, he paid too much for it. But, no matter. He left it with me, for safekeeping. He's on and off the island, and an empty house is no place for a valuable painting. What's to become of it now, I don't know. Would you like to see it?" He reached into a pocket, withdrew his cell phone, and scrolled through some photos.

The picture showed a typical Paul Henry landscape. The first thing you noticed was the low horizon; a third of the painting was devoted to a white sky with billowing cumulus clouds. Pale mountains held the center. The foreground occupied less than a quarter of the canvas—white cottages, patchy grass, and a bit of the bay. The palette was delicate and subdued, at least as the photo showed it. For color, you can't rely on a photo.

"It looks like a good example of his work," I said.

"It's hanging in my house at the moment. You're welcome to come see it."

"Thank you," I replied. "But what's the connection between the painting and your development plan? You said Bert bought it for the business."

Frank explained that Henry's work had become famous when it was used to popularize the west of Ireland as a tourist destination. In 1925 the railroad company used one of his paintings for a travel poster, and it became a national icon. So the idea was to promote their tourism project with a new Paul Henry poster. The original painting would grace the lobby of the planned hotel, and the poster would become a nationwide advertisement for the train ride.

Since seeing the Kildownet graves, I had a better understanding of why Bert's railway plan was controversial. "Frank, did my Uncle Bert know about that eerie prediction that the first and last trains to Achill would carry the dead?"

"Of course he knew. I told him about it myself."

"Well, didn't he, didn't you, wonder how it would go down with the public, getting them to take a ride on a train associated with death?"

"That was the whole point," Frank responded. "The prophecy was the thing. We'd use it to draw people to the island. Bert was a marketing genius, you know. He was sure people would line up to ride the 'Achill Death Train.' That's what he was going to call it. Chills and excitement, he said, that's what people want. There would be a guide on the train to tell the story of the prophecy and the disasters, and even special effects, maybe a sound and light show for the ride at night. 'It's the sizzle that sells the steak,' he used to say. Bert was going to do it up right."

I was too stunned to say anything. Toby, who has an expansive view of humankind and who is generally less appalled than I am by instances of bad taste, asked, "What's going to happen to the project now that Bert is gone?"

"I'll push on without him. I have to, don't I? I've invested too much to give up now."

A voice behind us boomed: "That's your plan, is it? I tell you, Hickey, if you try to push your shite death train down our throats, you'll end up like your partner." The speaker, a big man with a buzz cut and a red face, loomed over Frank's chair.

Frank shot to his feet, knocking over his glass. The black beer pooled on the table and flowed to the floor. "You'll not threaten me in a public house, Michael O'Hara. Are you confessing, then, to the killing of Bert Barnes?"

"Not a bit of it," the other retorted. "But there's many a man on this island who had reason to wish him harm. There were twenty-three God-fearing families waiting at the station to bury their dead on the day the first train to Achill arrived, and you want to capitalize on their grief. Have you no respect at all for the families? We're all still here, you know."

It suddenly became quiet. Gradually a chorus of grumbles arose from adjoining tables. "Some of my people were in those coffins," O'Hara went on. "And I mean to stop you."

"We're with you, Michael!" someone called out. "Can't you let the dead of Achill Island rest in peace?"

"Step away from me," said Frank, his chin leading, in defiance. "I want to get by."

"Oh, ya do, do ya?" said O'Hara, not moving. At which point everyone in the pub knew a donnybrook was at hand. A brawl is so common when the Guinness is flowing that the Irish coined a word for it.

I can't say who threw the first punch, but in a matter of moments the floor was a battlefield. Someone shoving to get close to Frank pushed my chair over, with me in it. That brought Toby to his feet, with arms churning. The man who had pushed me went down himself, but an ally of his jumped onto Toby's back. He must have thought Toby was a friend of Frank's, since we had been sitting at the same table. For a minute it looked like Toby was in trouble. He tried to break the hold but couldn't. He and his attacker halted, locked together by the force of opposing strength. Then, twisting to the left, Toby drove his right elbow into his assailant's gut. Toby pivoted and broke free.

Meanwhile, Frank Hickey was beset by a pile of men who jabbed at him like a pod of killer whales toying with their prey. Toby stepped in to even the odds, and bystanders joined the fray. The band struck up a tune, with the aim of calming people down, but the music only added to the tumult. Bobby Colman had chosen "Finnegan's Wake," a comic ballad celebrating the fun had by all when a brawl erupts at a drunkard's funeral. (That lad has a sense of humor, I thought.) By now, motive and grievance were overshadowed by the instinct to give blow for blow. Men were swinging at each other who had no reason for animus other than having been struck themselves. It became a general melee, which ended only with the arrival of the guard.

Garda Matt Mullen, who had questioned me at the Deserted Village after I found Bert's body, strode straight to the barman, who was quick to finger the instigators. After huddling with Frank Hickey and Michael O'Hara, the good-tempered guard made no arrests but gave them cautions. I tended to Toby, who had minor abrasions. Finally, Mullen suggested we all go home. I looked around for Angie, but she and Bobby Colman had already taken that advice.

7

BY NINE IN THE MORNING, Toby was still moaning under the covers, while I was in the kitchen in my sweats, hunched over a mug of Barry's Irish Breakfast made the cheater's way—with a tea bag, in a mug, without a teapot. My elbow was aching simply from falling out of the chair the night before, so I wasn't surprised that Toby was suffering in his sleep. I wondered whether to wake him for our lunch date with Maggie but decided I would go alone if he wasn't up by noon.

A short walk would fill out the morning nicely, and Angie would be the perfect partner, but her room was empty and her bed hadn't been slept in. When I knocked on our parents' door, Dad proved to be home alone. He surprised me by suggesting a walk to the beach at Dugort. Ordinarily, he's not a "go for a walk" kind of guy. For exercise, he bikes with Eddie and golfs with his buddies. This day, with no buddies in sight and Eddie back in the States tending to his pregnant wife, Dad picked me and the hills of Achill.

It was a soft day. By that, the Irish mean that the mist is almost drizzle, while the sky is light and cloudless. If you decide not to care about getting damp, it's fit weather for a walk. On days like this, the grass glows and the flowers pour color, but Dad seemed oblivious to the beauty. He walked mechanically, with eyes straight ahead. He spoke only to suggest how to skirt a plump ewe nursing her lamb in the road. Once in a while, one of us would point to a thatched roof or a bush blazing with fuchsia. After a mile of mostly downhill walking, we turned a corner and saw the sea at the end of the road. As we walked toward the beach, Dad reminisced, "Bert and I used to go out in a rowboat from a shore like that. See the black island out there? Ours was like that—it looked large from a distance, but it was just a big rock. And it looked jagged, like that one. Up close, though, the stone was washed smooth. Bert liked to jump from the boat onto the rock, leaving me to keep the damn boat from crashing."

"So you two were daredevils." I reached for Dad's shoulder, meaning to give him a playful pat, but he turned the other way and said, "Let's get back."

We began the uphill return. I felt I had to say something. "Dad," I began, "I'm sorry about Uncle Bert, really I am."

He kept looking at the road ahead, but he replied to me in a softer tone. "I know. I shouldn't have snapped at you yesterday. You're not responsible for how Mom feels about Bert."

"She feels that way because she takes your side. Mom just thinks that, between you and Bert, you always got the short end of the stick."

Dad halted and turned to me, with a look of disbelief. He brushed one hand across his face and then looked me in the eyes. "Nora, that's as far from the truth as it could be." He paused and turned back to his walking.

At last he continued. "Your mother knows this. You don't maybe, but Bert saved my life. I was the big brother. I was supposed to protect him. But that's not how it was. He saved me."

"When?"

"It was back home, in Arlington. You remember, I've shown you." I nodded, recalling a drive when Dad took us to see the old duplex where he grew up, in a working-class neighborhood just outside Boston.

"In the winter, we used to sneak off to Spy Pond. We could skate there if we got the guys together and shoveled when it snowed. We played hockey with brooms and a rock, nothing fancy. We weren't supposed to do it. The ice didn't always harden up well in the middle. But we took our chances."

"Grammy and Granddad didn't know?"

"Oh, no. Not until the accident. A kid named Johnny and I were chasing after a rock—the puck—and the ice gave under us. It happened in a crack. I remember the sound, and then the cold. I got pushed under Johnny, they say, as he grabbed the edge of the ice. Somebody stuck a broom out to him, handle first, and the guys held the brush end and pulled him forward. More ice cracked, they said, but they got him out. Everybody was so busy pulling Johnny away from the hole that nobody thought about me—except Bert. He was there, tagging along after me, as usual. He slid his skinny body to where I'd fallen through. He tells me he plunged his arm into the icy water, hoping I'd still be there. I was. I grabbed his hand, and I must have pulled him down. We were both deep under, grabbing at each other. The two of us almost drowned. Those guys saved us, though God knows how." He shook his head, looking mystified.

"Well, no wonder you felt grateful to him."

"Of course I did, but I felt guilty too. I never should have taken him out on the ice. It's my fault, what happened."

"It all turned out okay, though. Right?"

"No, it didn't. Bert got pneumonia, a really bad case. He nearly died. He was out of school for months, and when he went back, he was weak. You know, he always wanted to be a runner, and he had the build for it. But after the pneumonia, he couldn't run, he couldn't do any sports. His lungs were shot."

"Huh," I said. "And you think it was your fault."

"Not only his lungs. The kids bullied him after that. He didn't go out and play anymore. He didn't have friends. He sat at home, being miserable. He stayed like that, even after we moved to the beach house."

I couldn't reconcile Dad's portrait of his brother with the Uncle Bert I knew. He swaggered with self-esteem. As for friends, he knew everyone and everyone knew him, even, I imagined, on Achill.

"Uncle Bert never struck me as lacking confidence," I said. "Look how successful he was."

"College changed him. He came back a new man."

"Dad," I asked. "Did you give up going to college so that Bert could go instead?"

Dad gave a half smile. "Your mother's been talking to you." He paused and considered. "It's only half true. Bert pulled all A's in high school, and I was more of a jock. I could see he was made for the big time. I talked with your granddad about it, and we agreed that we should put our money into giving Bert his best shot."

"But it was at your expense. You missed out yourself."

"Maybe. Your mother thinks so. But now you can understand why I didn't begrudge Bert his success. I owed him, you see."

I squeezed his hand. "Thanks for telling me, Dad. I'm glad you did."

We reached the cottage too soon for me. I wanted to continue the conversation, but when we opened the door, there was Mom sitting at the kitchen table with her head down, drying her hair with a bath towel. She looked up and smiled a rueful smile. "You're as damp as I was an hour ago," she said. "You'll feel better after a shower." She rose and came to Dad, putting her hand on his cheek. They looked into each other's eyes, and their faces softened. They do that a lot, in good and bad times.

Mom glanced toward the door and asked, "Isn't Angie with you?"

"No, it's just us," I answered.

"I guess we each went our own way this morning," said Mom, resuming her toweling. I didn't correct her. She would find out soon enough that Angie had gone her own way last night. "There's a fresh pot of tea if you want some." She pointed.

"I think I'll take my shower first," said Dad, moving toward the bedroom.

"Thanks," I said. "I'll have some tea before I go for mine. Toby's probably still sleeping." I poured a cup and brought it to the table.

"Which way did you go?" asked Mom.

"We walked to the beach at Dugort. What about you?"

"I went to that little café down the road to pick up some pastries. There are sweet rolls in the bag on the counter."

I helped myself and sipped my tea while Mom finished toweling her hair. Some minutes passed in silence until she caught me looking at her.

"What?" she said.

"Nothing."

"It's not nothing. You're staring at me. I can see the little camera behind your eyes scrutinizing me, capturing my every twitch, storing it up for later analysis. Is that what you and Dad talked about on your walk—how's Mom handling all this? Is it creeping her out that somebody killed Bert when she's the one who hated him?"

"No. Mom! Dad wouldn't say that!"

"You're right. He wouldn't. But you would."

That stung.

"Look at you. You're recoiling from me."

"No, Mom, I just . . ."

She slapped her hand over mine and kept it there with pressure. She said, "I know you love me, Nora. But you're a woman. You think about people's feelings. We do, in a way Dad doesn't. And you're smart—too smart for your own good, sometimes."

My breastbone pulled inward. I couldn't talk. But I didn't pull my hand back. I didn't turn my head away.

"It's all right," she said. "Just don't pretend with me. Don't hide what you're thinking. We've got to stick together."

What did she mean by that?

"All right," she said, pulling her hand back. I was afraid to move mine. It still pressed on the table, and I was afraid it would shake if I raised it. "So what did you talk about, you and Dad?"

"It's like you said," I replied. "Dad was quiet, the way he always is when things are bad. I didn't push him. But he got to talking about when he was a boy in Arlington. He told me about the time that Bert saved his life when they were kids. I think Dad was trying to tell me why he felt so close to Bert in spite of the things Bert pulled when they were older—you know, the selfish stuff you always criticized him for."

"You're blaming me for criticizing him?"

"I'm not blaming. I just never had Dad's side of the story before."

"That's just it, it's a story. The fairy tale of the devoted brothers that never existed, Nora. I don't know how many times he's told me that 'he saved me' story. Dad should have gotten over his guilt toward Bert years ago. They were just kids when that accident happened. It was nobody's fault. And look at how Bert played him, after that."

"Okay, but you can't really blame Dad for taking Uncle Bert's side, even though he paid a price for it."

"We all paid a price for it. The whole family. Your father should have stood up to Bert instead of letting him act the cock of the walk and gobble up all the money and property."

Her voice became raspy, as the old grievance returned. I felt fear rising again in me, fear that Mom's resentment of Uncle Bert led to an outburst of deadly anger. Dad would never forgive her if it had.

We shared a minute of silence. Then I said, "Well, Bert is dead now, and we've got to deal with the police. How did your interview go at the station? Do you feel like talking about it?"

She draped the towel over the chair beside her and ran her fingers through her damp hair. "There isn't much to tell," she said. "They badgered me, but that got them nowhere. Police are the same all over. They try to trip you up and get you to admit things you didn't do."

"What do you mean?"

"Well of course they were worked up about the argument I had with Bert at the Jubilee, thanks to Laura telling them about it. But I said it was small potatoes, and they didn't get very far with it. And then they were on about whether I left the house the night he was killed, as if I needed an alibi."

"That's just a standard question they ask. Remember? We talked about that before the detectives arrived. You said you stepped out for a little air."

"Did I? I might have forgotten to tell them."

"You forgot to mention that you went outside for a walk?" I felt my pulse speeding up, but I kept my voice calm. "Mom, in case the question comes up again, you need to be clear about that point. What time was it when you went outside?"

"Oh, I don't know. It was after dinner, around eight or so."

"And how long were you gone?"
She shrugged.
"Mom, they'll want to know how long you were out of the house."
"Not long. I didn't go anywhere, just strolled a little around here."
"That's the main point. You were here all night."
"Of course I was."

I might have pressed her further but didn't. My palms felt clammy. "Mom, it's not a good idea to withhold information from the guards."

"I know that," she said. "Don't lecture me." She picked up the towel that was draped over the back of the chair and snapped it in the air.

I flinched. She was right. Who was I to lecture her? It was bad enough to withhold information from the police but worse to withhold hard evidence, and I was the one who was guilty of that.

Opening our cottage door, I smelled burnt toast. Toby had discovered that a couple of slices of Irish soda bread make a good breakfast, but they are hard to toast. Eaten fresh, the dark, dense bread is moist and delicious, but in the toaster it dries and crumbles before it's warmed through. If you insist on well-toasted bread, you're likely to overdo it. The garbage bin held a collection of charred slices.

Toby sipped his coffee and waved a finger. He looked pretty chipper for someone who had been in a barroom brawl the night before. He patted his mouth with a paper towel and said, "Frank Hickey called while you were out. He thanked me for coming to his aid at the pub last night. He wants to show you the Paul Henry painting."

"When?"

"Friday. He asked us to tea at his house. Is that okay?"

"Sure, but I can't think about it right now." I plopped myself down at the kitchen table and sighed.

"What's wrong?"

"It's Mom. What am I going to do?" I relayed the conversation we had just had. It was still acid in my mouth.

"You know," said Toby, "it's possible she's right. The police haven't been back. They must be moving on to other suspects."

"But what about her damned button? It means she was there. And if she was on the scene when Bert was killed, she may have left other physical evidence as well."

"Look. If you won't go to the police with the button, at least you've got to level with your mom. Maybe there's another explanation for how a button from her sweater ended up in the Deserted Village."

"Not just anywhere. At the crime scene. And I've been trying to bring up the subject every time I talk to her." I slumped down in the chair. "Damn it, I can't. I just can't do it."

"Is it because you're afraid of what you might find out?"

"Not just that. It's always been hard for me to confront her about anything."

"Do you want me to try?" asked Toby.

"No, I've got to do it. I just need more time."

"All right," said Toby. "But you don't have all the time in the world. It would be better for your mother to tell what she knows now rather than wait for the police to question her again."

"I know, I know."

Toby, looking doubtful, took an exasperated breath.

"Thanks for not pushing me more about the button," I said.

"The problem is that if you turned it in now, the police would be doubly suspicious. They'd want to know why you hesitated and whether you suspected your own mother."

"That wouldn't be good."

"No. We'd better get ready," said Toby, glancing at his watch. "We've got that lunch with Maggie and her friend."

Feeling low, I dragged myself off to the shower.

8

BY A QUARTER TO ONE, we were presentable, ready to meet Maggie for lunch in Keel, a few miles away. Mist wet the windscreen, but the midday sun was high, giving the road a white sheen. We didn't say much on the drive.

At our destination, the Beehive Coffee Shop and Crafts, we were told our table wasn't ready. A look around showed that tables were either occupied or uncleared. Two of the largest held the same family constellation: a mother, a granny, and a gaggle of tots. Older couples with English accents and Irish families on holiday filled out the room. Toby stood post at the hostess station to wait for a table and for Maggie; he knew I would want to tour the shop that occupied half the premises. As I did, my eye caught a sale sign on a rack of sweaters. Fingering a soft cardigan, I noticed the buttons. They were mother of pearl, not at all like Mom's silver button. I flicked the hangers back, one by one, checking out the buttons. Not one was silver. They were not so common as I wanted to think. I felt a flush of heat and an urge to leave, but soon Maggie and Mr. Ex arrived and I had a social event to get through.

Maggie's company always cheers me up, and meeting her ex intrigued me. Declan was tall, with dark hair graying at the temples. He had an angular face and sported a sparse goatee. Now, a beard is fine on a man, but a goatee is like a permanent ascot. In this and every other way possible, Declan took pains to distinguish himself from the crowd. Men in the restaurant were dressed casually—jeans, hoodies, and windbreakers suitable for the "soft day." Declan arrived in dark slacks, a white shirt, and a leather jacket that said casual chic rather than motorcycle grunge. I suppose he was good-looking, but in a self-dramatizing way. He smiled when Maggie introduced us, revealing smallish, pointed incisors.

Declan guided the conversation at lunch. He even selected our food, insisting that we must try the lamb stew, the special of the day. I had had plenty of lamb already; what with all the sheep on the island, it's a staple. I would have preferred a sandwich, but I felt obligated to join in the group order. I could see what Maggie meant when she called him controlling. Our talk ranged from eating on Achill (he approved of only two restaurants, this being one of them), to Irish theater (he spoke familiarly about current playwrights, claiming several as friends). When Toby mentioned he owned an antiques gallery, Declan gave instructions on which dealers he should visit in Westport and Castlebar.

When the topic turned to art, I thought I would have a chance to weigh in, but even here Declan held forth, mocking recent trends in the art market. He was scathing on the subject of "installations," which he called compendiums of junk. "A painter should paint," he proclaimed. "Installations are for plumbers." I had heard the line before. I confessed to Toby later that I felt like a student given the honor of dining with the eminent guest lecturer. Declan was proud that his Dublin gallery specialized in more traditional nineteenth- and early twentieth-century Irish painting. And that brought us to the events of the past week. When I mentioned the Paul Henry landscape that Uncle Bert had acquired to promote his tourist project, Declan's smooth urbanity gave way.

"Don't I know all about it?" he said. "I was desperate to get that painting, but he outbid me for it at Whyte's." Whyte's was the premier auction house in Dublin. Declan cleared his throat, a nervous tic. "I know he was your uncle, and I'm sorry for your family's trouble. But this isn't the first time something like that's happened. These rich Yanks come over with wads of money and drive up the prices of Irish paintings so we can't afford them anymore ourselves. They snap them up as ethnic badges to show off their Irish heritage. They have no real feeling for art. As a result, dealers like me have a hard time finding local inventory. But this time, I wanted that painting for myself."

"How much did it go for?" asked Maggie.

"Too much. The hammer price was two hundred thousand euros, not including the buyer's premium. I can't compete with that."

"Isn't that more than Paul Henry's work usually sells for?" asked Maggie.

"It used to be." Declan sighed. "A couple of his works recently sold for even more, one for half a million."

"What was it about that particular painting?" I asked. "My uncle's partner showed me a photo of it on his cell phone. It looks like a strong piece, but Henry painted other scenes quite like it, didn't he?"

"Similar, yes, but not identical. It's a great example of his ability to modulate tones and harmonize colors, painted two years after he arrived on Achill. And it's in pristine condition. But, more than that, it's a scene that has special meaning for me. It's the view from the house on Achill that my parents owned and where we spent our summers. I grew up with that view."

"Is that the place I'm staying at now?" asked Maggie.

"No, my parents' house burned down years ago. It was near Dooagh. That's why that painting means so much to me. I'd kill to have it." He caught himself, adding hastily: "I don't mean that literally, of course. Bad choice of words under the circumstances. Sorry."

How to reply to that? I didn't.

"Where's the painting now?" asked Maggie.

"It's at Frank Hickey's house," said Toby. "He's invited us to see it."

"Hmm. I wonder if he'll put it up for sale again," mused Declan.

"I don't think so," I replied. "He's planning to use the painting to advertise the new hotel and the steam railway."

"That remains to be seen," said Declan. "Word has it that the project was running into money problems well before your uncle was found dead. In fact, they say the partners had a falling out. If I were the guards, I'd be looking into that."

"There are plenty of people on Achill who resented Nora's uncle," Maggie pointed out.

"That's true, and I'm one of them," admitted Declan. "But now the project is Frank Hickey's to pursue or to give up. The whole island's wondering what he'll do."

For a while, we ate in silence. The lamb stew was savory, and the wine that Declan had ordered to go with it was a perfect match for the dish, but grim talk makes a poor meal.

"If I could change the subject," Toby began, addressing Declan with a bit of mischief in his eyes, "Maggie tells us—" But he was interrupted by a warning kick under the table, which resulted in a midsentence pivot. I knew what he was up to. He was dying to ask about the Achill swingers' club. Declan waited for Toby to continue.

"Uh, Maggie tells us we've been lucky with the weather so far. Only morning showers," Toby finished lamely.

Declan sensed he was missing the subtext and turned to Maggie for enlightenment. She gave the slightest of shrugs. "That's so," he agreed. "Achill's been on its good behavior, but watch out, she's as changeable as our woman here." He turned a hand toward Maggie, without looking at her. "One day she's warm, the next day she's cold."

"Get on with you," said Maggie dismissively.

Toby caught my eye, looking miffed. He would find a way to wheedle the information he wanted from Maggie's ex, one way or another. For now, though, he beckoned for the bill.

After lunch we headed for the market in Achill Sound to pick up provisions for supper. Toby and I do the cooking together. I defer to his superior skills, which means that he plans the menu (after all, a chef is inspired when he's cooking what he likes), does most of the grocery shopping (he doesn't trust anyone else to pick the best produce), and sets the strategy (cooking techniques, order of preparation). I make suggestions, follow orders, solve problems, and serve. That evening we put the system to work at Mom and Dad's cottage and produced a meal that contented everyone: broiled salmon with caper-butter sauce, pureed peas, and a salad of chopped celery and raisins. Nobody had to know that the salmon and peas started frozen or that the salad had no lettuce because the greens at the grocers were brown. We topped it all off with ginger cake made by the grocer's wife.

The atmosphere at dinner was tense, without much talking. I summarized our lunch with Maggie and Declan, but my account was incomplete. If we weren't going to talk about Uncle Bert's death, we certainly weren't going to talk about Maggie's sex life.

Over dessert, Mom cracked the shell. "We were with Laura and Emily this afternoon."

"Oh?" said Angie. "Was there a wake I didn't know about?"

"You'll know if there's a wake," Dad said. "The body hasn't been released. Anyhow, the wake will be in Wellesley."

"That makes sense," Angie said. "That's where their friends are, and Grammy." As if choreographed, we all put our forks down. Grammy. We looked at Dad, and he knew what we were thinking.

"We called Grammy, from Laura's. It was tough."

"We'll call too," I promised Dad. Her family needs to get home to her, I thought. And yet we couldn't, not till the investigators were finished with us.

Dad pushed away his half-eaten cake.

Angie left to join Bobby Colman at his band rehearsal, and Mom asked me to do the dishes with her so Toby and Dad could play chess in the other room. I hoped that Mom wanted to talk, over the suds.

As we cleared the table, Mom took the lead. "I want to ask you about Angie," she said. "What's going on with this Bobby?"

"I think they're flirting with each other." That was all I knew for sure.

"It's gone beyond that," Mom announced. She kept me waiting for explanation as she leaned over to put detergent in the dishwasher. Using gestures to tell me to rinse the dishes and hand them to her, she explained, "Our little Angie spent the night out. We didn't see her till we got back from Laura's." There was amusement in Mom's voice, not the worry I had expected.

Now, Mom's not prudish, but she's always been protective of Angie, so I was a little confused. "You're not concerned, then?" I asked.

"Maybe, maybe not. This could be a good thing. Angie's not cut out for the religious life. Better she should realize it herself than be kicked out later." We were getting into a quick rhythm with our dishes assembly line, even as we discussed a hot topic.

"Kicked out? Where do you get that idea?" I asked.

"You said yourself, last summer—her mother superior watched Angie fall in love with that French policeman. She's only stringing Angie along, waiting till she comes to her senses."

"Her senses seem to be the problem, actually." We laughed, and I relaxed with Mom for the first time since the murder.

"What do you think of this new boyfriend?" Mom asked. "Worth leaving the convent for?"

I had to ponder that. At last I said, "Worth something. He seems like a good person, but that's just a first impression."

"I wouldn't want her to get her heart broken again," Mom said, more seriously.

"They both have to know it's a summer romance. We'll be gone as soon as we're allowed. But you're right. Even a summer romance should tell Angie she'll never be ready for celibacy."

"Never," Mom said quietly. "She's never going to take those vows, and she never should." Then, in a confidential tone, she said, "Why don't you get some time alone with her tomorrow? Maybe you can get her to see the light."

"I don't know, Mom. She hasn't asked my opinion."

"You're the only one she'll listen to now. Dad and I have said all we can. You have to help us."

"It's not my place. I'm her sister. I've got to be on her side, whatever she wants." The minute I said it, I knew I had laid bait for a fight.

"You think I'm not on her side? I'm her mother. I've been on her side every day of her life."

"I know that."

"No, you don't know. You've been away from home too long. You didn't watch her growing up, too beautiful and sweet to be safe in this world. It's been a struggle, watching over her and protecting her from being taken advantage of. It's your turn to help us, with this convent nonsense."

I recognized the impulse to steer Angie away from trouble; I've felt it myself, many times, but I've been trying to step back and let Angie be herself. She doesn't need family supervision anymore; in fact, she has a right to resent it.

"Angie's future will take care of itself," I asserted, with more confidence than I felt. "We've got our own troubles to deal with—Uncle Bert's murder. That's what we should be talking about."

Mom slammed the bottom rack of the dishwasher back, and it jammed. "Uncle Bert! It's still always about him." She jerked the rack back and forth till it fell into its groove with a force that made the dishes clank. "There's no point in talking about something we know nothing about," she said. "The police will have to look to the locals." She dried her hands on the dish towel and put it down. "If you ask me, they won't find out who did it. Every man and his brother hates Bert—here, at home, wherever. By now they probably have a dozen suspects. They won't need to bother about us."

I don't know if she saw my skeptical look, but she backed away from the sink and said, "Would you finish up here? I'm going to our room to write Grammy a letter." She walked to the bedroom door but stopped to call back, "We'll see you at supper tomorrow. Dad and I need some time to ourselves."

Mom didn't come out of her room, even when Toby and I called good-bye.

9

IN THE MORNING, Inspector O'Donnell called and asked if I would meet him at the garda station in Achill Sound. He said he had "just a few additional questions" about my statement, and it shouldn't take long. The station was in a small, yellow house just before the bridge to the causeway. When I arrived, Garda Mullen greeted me and offered me a cup of tea. He had to climb a flight of creaky wooden stairs to fetch it. "I don't want to put you to the trouble," I said, but he waved me off. The inspector was waiting in the main sitting room on the ground floor, leaning back on two legs of a cane-backed chair.

"Thank you for coming."

"Not at all. I'm happy if I can be of help."

"Then I'll get right to the point." The inspector brought his chair back to its upright position. "I want to ask you again about your family and your uncle. There wasn't much love lost between your family and Bertram Barnes. Am I correct?"

I tried to stay composed. "Actually, my father was quite fond of his brother."

"Yes, but I've been told that your mother and your uncle didn't get on. Is that the case?"

It was best to tell the truth—but not necessarily all of it. "Uncle Bert was not my mother's favorite person, if that's what you're asking." I stopped there. Don't say more than you have to. Be direct. Answer the question.

The inspector jotted a note on his pad. "What reservations did your mother have about your uncle?"

I glanced at my face in a small mirror opposite me on the wall. I looked strained. "I think she felt that he didn't treat my father as well as he should have. Lots of families have those kinds of issues."

"I understand there was a public quarrel between your mother and your uncle at a family celebration in Galway just before you arrived on Achill. Can you tell me what that was about?"

I wondered if this all came from Laura and Emily or if he had been talking to people in Galway. I took a slow breath to keep myself calm. "There's been a disagreement about what will happen to the family home when my grandmother dies. It's more about fairness than about money. That's what they were arguing about. I wouldn't make too much of it."

"According to witnesses, your mother was quite angry." The inspector flipped a few pages on his pad and read from one of them. "She was heard to say, 'If you get that house, I hope you die in it.' Is that correct?"

So the inspector's team *had* been talking to the guests at the Jubilee. "I didn't hear the whole argument," I said. "But families quarrel all the time and people get angry. Sometimes they say things they don't mean literally. I'm sure you know that, Inspector."

"Even so, when one of the parties to a quarrel turns up dead two days later, it raises questions. Particularly if the circumstances suggest a crime of passion rather than a premeditated attack."

"I'm not sure I follow you."

"Someone who planned in advance to kill your uncle—say someone who wanted to stop the railway project—would have brought a weapon to the scene. But whoever killed him used a rock, picked one up and struck him, perhaps on a moment's impulse. That suggests a personal rather than a political motive."

Now I was really worried. O'Donnell was implying that my mother had a motive to murder Uncle Bert, a passionate anger against him, and the means, a simple rock. The one element missing from the frame was opportunity, but she may have had the opportunity too. What would happen if Mom's alibi came into doubt? What evidence might the inspector have? Could they get fingerprints from a rock? Had the tech team come up with anything? There was the button, of course, but Toby and I were the only ones who knew about that. So far.

O'Donnell was waiting for me to reply. "I don't think my mother or anyone else in our family had anything to do with what happened to my uncle. Do you have any evidence that suggests they did?"

The inspector folded his hands in his lap. "The investigation is ongoing. I'm simply considering the possibilities."

"Maybe you should concentrate on the threats made against my uncle by people on the island. That's where you'll find the answers."

"So you've said. I can assure you we are following all leads." He tilted his chair back again.

I waited for him to continue, but he said nothing more. "Is there anything else?" I asked.

"Just that for now."

"Then may I go?"

"Yes. We'll talk again."

Toby was waiting on a bench outside the cottage when I got back. "How'd it go?" he asked.

I gave him an account. "I'm worried, Toby. It doesn't look good for Mom."

There was still a long afternoon ahead of us. I had made a walking date with Angie to see one of the island's megalithic tombs and hoped that would take my mind off the investigation. Being with Angie always boosts my mood. Toby decided to hunt for antiques for his shop back home.

I had found a paperback on the island's archaeology and folklore and was deep into a chapter on megalithic tombs when Angie came to the door.

"Ready?" she asked.

"I'm ready, but I wasn't sure if you'd be coming. I thought you might be off with your music man," I said.

"He's got a day job," she retorted. "'Sheep, shearing, and shite,' he calls it." Her dreamy smile didn't go with the earthy terms for Bobby's work. "So tell me, Professor, what's this megalith we're going to?"

I did my best to be upbeat. "It's a prehistoric monument. 'Megalith' just means 'huge stone.' Achill has more of them than anywhere else in Ireland, and we have one of the best practically on our doorstep. You're going to love it. Think warlords and wizards and human sacrifice. Well, not really. Human sacrifice was a Mayan thing. It should be impressive, though."

"How old is this megalith supposed to be?"

"They say it goes back five thousand years, when people first settled along the side of the mountain. They planted fields to the east of the village, and beyond the fields they buried their dead. And they built these tombs out of gigantic stones."

"I'll have to take pictures. Sister Glenda would love this." Sister Glenda, the mother superior at Angie's convent back home, is an expert on the relationship between art and spirituality. The salient fact for the Barnes family is that she may have a say as to Angie's future. Then again, so may Bobby the folk-singing shepherd.

Setting that thought aside, I assessed Angie's mood. She looked ready to go. Without further talk, I found her a sunhat and we were off.

The day was bright and windy, whipping the grasses on the lands beyond our cottages. At one time there must have been a footpath between this hill and "the field of the giants," as some called the site of the tombs, but the way I knew was the road we had taken to the Deserted Village. The route gave a fair sample of the island's beauties. Our cottages sat at the same height on the mountain as the Deserted Village—high enough to give us a panoramic view of ocean, shore, and mountain. The sweep of Keel beach anchored a wide bay, with low cliffs and a small island off to the west. In the distance, gulls hovered over the water, seeking balance as the wind whipped gusty currents. To the east, spectacularly high cliffs extended for miles, edging the great mass of mountain that ended at Dooega Head. Between us and the sea lay the meadows used by Bobby and his fellow sheep farmers.

The road downhill from the cottages afforded no such views. In Ireland, roads tend to be bordered with hedges masking stone walls, posing a hazard for tourists driving on "the wrong side" of the road. Here, thick hedges dripped fuchsia blossoms, each a delicate red bell with a violet interior. By some trick of the sun, the brilliant hedges grew only on the left side of the road. The right verge was thick with wildflowers like purple lupine and thistle, alternating with untended plantings of calla lily and sea rose. I kept my eyes on the right, looking for the megalithic tombs, and at last I spotted the inconspicuous brown sign that said Tuama Meigiliteach.

The site was protected by a turnstile, a gate with four revolving arms. Any child could find a way through it, but not a dimwitted sheep. Beyond the gate, a grassy lane led up Slievemore Mountain. There wasn't a big stone in sight, never mind a megalith. But, keeping faith, we followed the not-so-well-worn path up and up. Finally, we mounted a rise, from which we could see, at a distance, a hem of gray, pebbly ground below the rock face of the mountain. Nearer us, perhaps a football field away, lay a pile of rocks, white in the sunshine. They might have been random stones thrown down by nature, except that the path led directly to them.

"That must be it," I said.

"No way," Angie scoffed. "You said 'megalith' meant 'huge stone.' I've seen bigger end tables."

"Let's see what it looks like when we get close."

It was farther away than it looked, and yet it didn't gain much in the impression of height as we got closer. From a jumble of boulders scattered on the ground, there emerged a central form, a stolid table, perhaps an altar. The tabletop was supported by three bulky stones, pressing against each other. They didn't look cut by man. The central stone was round, bearing its share of the weight on its curved top. The stones on either side were shaped like giant crystals. These three unmatched pillars held up a stone slab, the capstone, less than a foot thick but with a surface of at least six by five feet. I approached, bent down, and peered through the cracks between the supporting stones. What lay beyond was shadowy, difficult to read, but it wasn't pitch dark.

"Let's go around," I said. It seemed right to confront this mystery together. To the left of the stonework, we stumbled down the rubble of an ancient staircase carpeted with moss. Angie reached the other side before I did.

"It's a little building!" she shouted. It looked low for a building, but as I moved around, I saw that we had been looking at the back wall of a stone hut with three sides and a flat roof that projected out over a sunken patio. I moved carefully, afraid I might trip over one of the lower stones that bordered the patio. I couldn't resist the urge to drop to my knees and crawl under the roof stone. A child or a small adult would be able to sit in there, either looking through the open front "door" toward the mountain or turned around to look through the chinks, as if they were windows, for a view of the sea. Being too tall for that, I could only lie on my back, feeling swaddled in stone. Then the obvious hit me. This is a grave. I am the corpse. This is the megalithic tomb.

My reverie was shattered by an angry shout: "What in God's name are ya playin' at? This is a sacred site. Come out from there, will ya?"

The querulous voice was followed by Angie's nervous one. "Um, Nora. There's somebody here who wants to speak with you."

Well, that much I already knew. I scrambled out as quickly as I could. Before me stood a small, emaciated man, leaning on a homemade walking stick. His hair was long and white, as was his beard. His eyes were stern, barely blue, almost colorless. He was dressed in shabby clothes, too thin for the windy day. Angie backed away.

"I meant no disrespect," I said evenly. "I'm sorry if I offended you. I thought we were alone." Where indeed had he come from, and how was it that we hadn't noticed him during our approach? The surrounding terrain was flat and open, with unblocked views in every direction.

"It's not me who's offended. You ought to have respect for the old ones."

"I'm truly sorry. Please accept my apology."

He stared at me for a long minute. "Well, now, I do see shame in your face, so I'll take it you're repentant. Tourists from America, are ya?"

"Yes, that's right. We wanted to learn something about the megalithic tombs."

"Is it to learn? Then you're not like some. The lookers, I call 'em. They look but don't see. As blind as the herring leaping in Dingle Bay."

"My name is Nora, and this is my sister, Angie."

He nodded. "Some call me the Prophet of Dugort. But the name is Brian."

"How do you do? I'm sorry too," said Angie, coming closer. "Who are the old ones?"

"The ancestors," he replied. "Mine, and yours as well if you have Irish blood in your veins."

"We do," she said. "Our grandparents on my father's side."

The strange man pointed to the tomb, with an expansive gesture. "Mind you, 'tis our people built these tombs and who were buried here. And if their bodies are long gone, their spirits are still present."

"Do you really think so?" asked Angie. "That's something I've been wondering about. If our ancestors lived here five thousand years ago, they couldn't have been Christian, because Christianity didn't exist yet, so they must have been pagan, but did they have their own religion?"

Brian planted his staff in front of him and leaned back on his heels. "The Irish religion is all one, girl. 'Tis all one!" he remonstrated. "The ancients were holy. And later, didn't the priests hold services here when the people were forbidden by the English to practice their religion? Why, they used this very capstone as their altar."

"You mean the priests said Mass here?" asked Angie.

"They did, surely, in secret."

"Was that during the time of the Penal Laws?" I asked. The Penal Laws were a set of anti-Catholic measures imposed by the British in the eighteenth century and much resented. Their intention was to convert the population to Protestantism.

"Aye, but we kept our religion alive. We used our ingenuity to outwit our enemies." He nodded. "It's been that way for centuries. Have ya heard about the landlord who went from farm to farm in the time of the Famine evicting the poor who couldn't pay their rent? One day he was found dead, but the police could never prove a crime because there wasn't a mark on his body. Ye see, someone had forced a loaf of Irish brown bread down his throat, choking him. But there was no trace left of it by the time the man was found. The rats ate what the body didn't digest. I call that ingenuity." The old man pounded his staff on the ground for emphasis and continued. "Ingenuity and prophecy. Those are the greatest gifts of our people."

Angie's curiosity was piqued. "Like the prophecy of iron carriages coming to Achill carrying the bodies of the dead?" Angie had been fascinated by that tale when I related it to her.

"And didn't it happen just as my kinsman, Brian the Red, foretold centuries ago?"

"It's the most amazing story I ever heard," said Angie.

"If it isn't true, it isn't day," snorted Brian, pointing toward the sun. "It came to pass exactly as foretold."

"I believe you," Angie said. "Were you named after him? The prophet, I mean."

The stranger seemed to relax now that he had a willing listener. "I was named Brendan, after my father, at birth. But when I was a boy they started to call me Brian when they discovered I had the gift of seeing things that no one else saw."

"What kind of things?" she pursued.

He tucked his chin into his chest and glowered. Satisfied that she wasn't mocking him, he resumed. "One day, when I was ten years old, and the sea was calm and as flat as a looking glass, I looked out and saw black clouds and a desperate storm and three men struggling in the water. The next day Paddy McGann's curragh washed up empty on the beach of Keel and his body the week after, and they never did find his brothers, Sean and Joseph, who had gone out with him that time to pull the nets."

Angie's eyes opened wider, but our visitor unnerved me. I'm pretty much a doubter when it comes to the supernatural, while Angie has always been drawn to the uncanny. As a child she believed absolutely in angels—still does, as a matter of fact. I suppose many people do, but Angie's also tried psychic readings, tarot cards, and New Age crystals, not to mention the summer she spent in an ashram led by a self-styled swami from Pawtucket. Mom thought that her tryout with the convent was just the latest in a series of spiritual enthusiasms, which was one of the reasons it wouldn't last. In any case, Angie was captivated by the stranger's account.

Grasping his walking staff with both hands, he leaned forward and dropped his voice, as if sharing a secret. "Aye, all my life I've had the gift, but it's been no use to me. On Saturday last, didn't I see the ghost train hurtling through the night, carrying its dead passengers, wailing and moaning, the poor souls. And the next morning they found the body of that Yank who said he would bring the old steam railway back to Achill. I reckon he was disturbing their rest. Now he's among them."

This was unsettling to say the least. "You're talking about our uncle!" Angie blurted in consternation.

The old man's face registered surprise. "In that case, I'm sorry for your trouble. But a warning for ya then. It isn't over."

"What do you mean by that?" I said. Angie retreated a few steps.

He turned toward me. "This morning before I left my bed I saw the Achill train again. The spirits on board were clawing at the windows." He held me in a penetrating gaze. "There will be another death."

"There will? Who?" cried Angie.

He didn't reply but simply said, "That's the reason I've come here today, to pay my respects and say a prayer."

That was enough of the uncanny for me. I said, as politely as I could, "Angie, let's go and leave this gentleman to his prayers. I'm sorry if we disturbed you, sir. Come." I took her hand and tugged. Reluctantly she followed, and we started back down the trail. Angie wanted to talk, but I shushed her until we had put some distance between ourselves and the self-styled prophet. I turned back once to look, but I saw no one. He must have stepped behind the tomb; he couldn't have disappeared that quickly in the bare terrain.

We walked as fast as we could until we regained the road leading back to our cottages. "I'm scared," Angie said.

"Maybe that's what he meant to do, scare us."

"Why would he do that? He doesn't know who we are."

He does now, I thought to myself. "Maybe he doesn't like tourists. He said as much, remember? Besides, I don't really believe in prophecies."

"Well, maybe you should. How do you account for the vision he had before Uncle Bert was killed?"

"I can't. But how do we know he had that vision before the murder rather than after it? Maybe he read about it in the paper and it gave him bad dreams."

"You know what, Nora? To me, he sounded sincere. What about Brian the Red predicting the coming of the railway to Achill and saying that its first passengers would be corpses?"

"I don't know, Angie. Maybe it's just a folktale."

"And maybe there are some things that can't be explained," said Angie, stopping in the road. "Now we have a prediction about the future. He says there's going to be another death."

"People die every day," I said. "There's always going to be another death."

Toby pooh-poohed the account of our experience at the tomb, though he liked the story of the landlord who had been dispatched by a loaf of bread. He had enjoyed a tiring but successful day antiquing, having scored a pair of brass carriage lanterns and a trove of saleable bric-a-brac. The find that most excited him, however, was an Irish wake table from the 1840s. I had never heard of one. As he explained it, the table was sturdy enough to support a coffin during a wake. This one was mahogany and had elegant carving on the legs. With its leaves down, it would hold a coffin nicely; with its leaves up, it could serve year-round as an attractive dining table. Toby was confident that as an unusual piece it would fetch a good price at home. To me it sounded macabre. "I wouldn't want to eat on a table where a body's been laid out," I said.

"Me neither," Toby allowed, "but someone will buy it." He paused. "Speaking of bodies—think live ones this time—what about checking out that swingers' club Maggie told you about? Just out of curiosity. I was thinking about it while I was driving around the island today."

"What a segue to get to your favorite subject," I marveled, "going from death to sex!"

He looked a bit cowed. "Better than the other way around."

"True enough," I said. "It's time for bed."

10

THE NEXT DAY, hearing nothing further from the inspector about the investigation, I took Toby on a long walk, to shake off the ghosts. He had asked for a tour of the megalithic tomb, but I just couldn't. I proposed instead that we drive north above Keel and follow a path from the beach through the bogs. The guidebook promised a lively stream fringed thickly with flowers, the contrast of bare, black bogs, and the grandeur of walking toward mountains with the ocean at our backs. All this was delivered with white, billowing clouds blowing fast across the sky. Toby tramped the trail energetically, and I tried to keep pace. But from my hips to my feet, I felt weighted. I gave it my best, but Toby could tell.

"Too much today," he said.

He understood how I was feeling—my shock at finding Bert dead, my concern for my mother, all the emotions tangled up inside me. I knew the guards were working diligently behind the scenes and wondered if they had turned up anything new. I carried Mom's button with me everywhere, afraid that in the cottage it would be vulnerable to discovery. I kept fingering it in my pocket nervously. Toby noticed my jitters. He rubbed my back lightly and said, "Let's slow down."

The path turned away from the bogs toward the sea. As we descended, my breath came back and my limbs grew lighter. By the end of the walk, I was ready for another, but Toby called for lunch at the beach café. "Famous for their double-chocolate cake," Toby said. He knew I couldn't resist that.

Toby and I love an hour of reading after lunch. Since Mom and Dad's car was gone and we didn't see Angie about, we grabbed our chance. Toby took the bedroom, which meant either a good read or a good nap. I confiscated a book from the living room—my first Maeve Binchey—and took the couch. I was settled into marriage on Tara Road and beginning to sniff adultery when a knock on the window made me lose my place. It was Angie, waving at me in an odd, backhanded gesture, which I interpreted as a request to be let in. Once through the door, she continued waving her hand back and forth, first in front of her face in peek-a-boo style, and then at hip height, as if drying fingernail polish.

"Is that a jig that you learned from Bobby?" I asked.

She giggled. "It's something that I got from Bobby. Look!" She thrust her right hand toward my chest. A silver band with a raised heart shone on her ring finger.

I flopped back on the couch pillows, and Maeve Binchy fell to the floor.

"Don't say it!" Angie said. "It's not an engagement ring."

"Then what is it?"

"A friendship ring. See—it's a heart held by two hands."

"I know about claddagh rings," I said, "and I know they're engagement rings."

"You're out of date, cupcake. They've been used as engagement rings, but now they're friendship rings too. Some people even buy them for themselves, to show they're Irish. The heart means love, of course, and the crown on the heart is for loyalty, and the hands mean friendship."

"Methinks the lady doth protest too much," I muttered.

"I'm not protesting anything. There's nothing wrong with exchanging friendship rings."

"Exchanging?"

"Yes. Bobby gave me this one, and I gave him one."

"So this isn't Bobby's grandmother's heirloom claddagh ring that he's been saving for the right girl?"

Angie looked put out. "Maybe I *am* the right girl! And maybe not. Whatever."

I told myself to be nice, and I said, "It's very pretty. Where did you get it—them?"

"At the craft shop across from the town hall at Achill Sound. Bobby went to school with the owner. He fitted us and explained how to wear them. They're a local tradition, you know. Claddagh's not that far from here. See, I'm wearing it on my right hand, which means it is *not* an engagement ring. But the point of the heart is toward my waist, which means . . ."

"You finally ended up in the sack."

She blushed by way of confirmation. "It means the wearer is in a relationship."

"Aha!" I said. "So more than just friendship."

Angie pouted. "Why do you always have to pin me down? I like my ring. Bobby likes his ring. We like having rings together. Period."

"And are you planning to send a picture of it to Sister Glenda along with the other snapshots of your trip?"

"I don't need to be reminded of the convent, okay? I'm supposed to be testing how I feel about giving up sex before I make a commitment to the order, that's what Sister said. To see if it's the right choice for me. So I'm testing." She grinned.

"Well, I'm glad you are," I said. It was good to know that Angie was monitoring her feelings, but I couldn't help joshing her. "Testing—one, two, three," I teased, miming an announcer talking into a microphone. That broke the tension and we both laughed. The giver of the ring arrived soon after, which kicked up a fuss of tea-making.

"Don't be troubling yourself," Bobby said, while seating himself at the table. From that vantage point, he watched contentedly while Angie put water in the kettle and brought out a box of Mikados. Now, there was a sign of assimilation. After only a week in Ireland, Angie was addicted to these little wands of biscuit and chocolate. And here she was sharing her stash with her "friend." I caught her placing her right hand on the table, next to Bobby's, to create a display of the twin rings. His was the masculine counterpart to hers, with a thicker band showing a raised heart topped by a crown and supported by clasped hands. Bobby turned to look at her, and they shared what they thought was a private smile.

Then Bobby sat up straight, as if waking himself up, and put a question to me. "Did our girl tell you she's going to be a star?"

"With Angie, you have to be ready for anything," I said. "Star of what?"

"We're putting on *The Playboy of the Western World* to kick off our summer festival on Sunday, and we need a fill-in for one of the cast who just dropped out. Angie's agreed to take her place.

"But that's only a few days from now. How's she going to learn the part?"

"It won't be hard," Angie replied. "I've just got a walk-on part with a couple of lines. It'll be fun."

Angie's always been attracted to the theater. All through school she tried out for plays and usually managed to get chosen for a role. It started with *Eat Your Veggies* in the first grade, when she played a carrot. (Angie was always the tallest girl in her class.) So it wasn't too surprising that she would volunteer to step in at the last minute at the request of her new beau. "Bobby plays the hero," she enthused. "He's going to help me rehearse."

"Well, good luck," I said.

"You're supposed to say, 'break a leg.' That's what theater people say." She beamed.

"Do you know the play?" asked Bobby. "It's by John Millington Synge, our greatest playwright."

"I've never seen it, but I've always been intrigued by the title."

With the pride of the newly informed, Angie took it upon herself to explain. "It doesn't mean 'playboy' in, like, a rich guy who runs around with a lot of babes. It means more of a rogue and a braggart. And the 'western world' refers to right here. It's a play about the west of Ireland."

"That's right," added Bobby. "It's set on the coast of County Mayo."

"It's about a stranger who comes to town and claims he's running from the police," continued Angie. "His name is Christy Mahon—that's Bobby—and when he tells his story, the people take him for a great outlaw, and all the girls chase after him."

I must have looked puzzled.

"It's a comedy," said Bobby.

I could use a comedy right about now, I thought. "Well, you've definitely got my interest. I can't wait to see it."

"Then we better get on with our rehearsal," said Bobby. "Will you excuse us?"

I left them together, huddled over their paperback editions of the play. Angie seemed happier than she had been in a long time.

There's a busy little butcher shop in a small strip of stores at the entrance to Achill Sound. I suggested we go there to get meat for dinner, preferably something other than lamb. I had started to feel globules of lamb fat congealing in my blood. Before we left the cottage, Toby said hello to the budding thespians and was treated to a display of their new rings. "Bobby seems nice enough," he said as we drove through the low-lying, monochrome bog lands. "Maybe this time it'll work out."

"I hope so. Angie's had too many disappointments with men."

"I have a feeling," said Toby, "this time might be different."

"From your mouth to God's ear," said I.

Twenty minutes later, as we approached our destination, we encountered an angry group of people milling about the small parking lot in front of the butcher shop. They were blocking the entrance, so we pulled to the curb. Within moments, the restive gathering spilled out of the parking lot and into the street. Protestors brandished signs. Save Our Greenway, said one. No to the Achill Steam Train, said another.

Save Our Cycling Path, Keep Achill Green, said a third. Some of the demonstrators had bicycles by their sides; others carried walking sticks and had backpacks. Passersby stopped on the sidewalk to see what was going on. A buzz of approval arose when a red-haired woman and a burly man stepped out of the shop and moved to the front of the crowd. The man I recognized as the instigator of the brawl in the Annexe pub; he was red-faced Michael O'Hara. Today he wore a butcher's apron. The woman beside him was striking: tall and slim, with fiery red hair flowing down her back. She wore a green cloak around her shoulders, which reminded me of Maud Gonne, the beautiful Irish revolutionary who cast a spell on Yeats. She must have mounted a box or platform of some kind, for in a moment she was elevated above the crowd.

"Let's see what's happening," said Toby. He slowly drove forward past the blocked entrance and found a parking space down the street. We walked back and stood at the edge of the crowd to listen.

The speaker was inveighing against Uncle Bert's idea to reconvert a section of the old Achill railbed to its original purpose. Just a few years ago, she reminded the protestors, the rails had been torn up and the trackway transformed into a hiking and bicycle trail for the enjoyment of all. What once was the Great Midlands Railway was now the Great Western Greenway, an environmental gem stretching some twenty-six miles from Achill to Westport. The disused rail route had been granted a second lease on life and was now a path for nature lovers on foot or on bike.

"Our greenway is known throughout the country," the woman shouted. "But today it is threatened. Greedy businessmen want to convert it to a train ride for personal profit. The death of the project's top developer hasn't stopped them. The plan is still moving forward, led by his partner and their rich backers. It's up to the people of Achill to stop them!"

"We will!" shouted one belligerent man. "Frank Hickey will get what's coming to him!"

I grasped Toby's arm at the elbow.

"We don't want that kind of talk," the speaker admonished. "I understand your anger. But we're taking our grievance to court. That's why I'm asking for your donations. Solicitors cost money, and you can be sure the developers have plenty of that." She scanned the faces in the crowd and continued. "We've already seen how easily green belt protection can be circumvented. The county planning committee has shown just how susceptible it is to business interests by giving its approval for a disgraceful scheme, supposedly to increase tourism on Achill. Sure, their decision's no surprise. Didn't money tempt Judas to betray the Lord? I'd like to know whose hands were crossed with silver before the planning committee got flexible."

"Dead right!" yelled the butcher.

"The applicants," she went on, "have influence and large financial resources, and we're nothing but a bunch of boggers and fishers to them. And yet, we've pushed back. We've spoken at council meetings, we've sent a petition, and we've held demonstrations. Now legal action is required if our greenway is to be preserved."

"And if legal action doesn't work, we'll damn well block the construction. We'll down the site!" shouted another voice.

"Save our greenway!" The chant picked up with people standing near the speaker, and it spread throughout the group. Pretty soon everyone was chanting, the notable exceptions being us.

We were spotted by Michael O'Hara, who pointed in our direction. "That fella in the back is a friend of Frank Hickey," he called out. "He's no friend of ours." That prompted a collective grumble of resentment. A man standing next to us turned to Toby and said, "You're not welcome here." Another man began pushing his way toward us.

Toby said in an even voice, "We're going." He tugged me gently into the street. The men let us pass, but several rough-looking boys followed us to our car. I said to Toby, "So much for the butcher's." That evening we made do with soup.

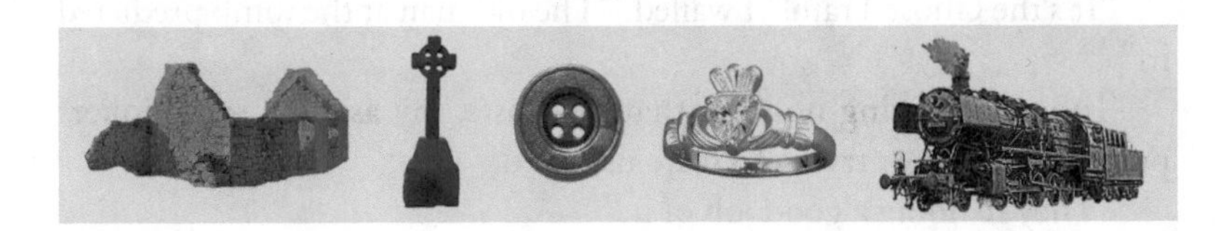

11

At first I thought I was dreaming. The clock on the night table read 3:20. And there it was again—a screech of metal wheels, the hoot of a whistle, the rush of something mighty passing by, and the distinctive rhythm of clickety-clack, clickety-clack that could mean only one thing—a train hurtling through the night. But there hadn't been a train on Achill for eighty years.

Toby woke up too. "What the hell was that?" He threw the blanket aside and swung his legs over the side of the bed. The racket of a roaring train repeated at a volume that suggested it was close. I grabbed my robe and followed Toby to the kitchen, the side of the house from which the sounds were coming. We peered out the window. Outside, the grounds were enveloped in fog, through which black patches of sky were just visible. It was impossible to distinguish anything on the ground except for a green glow in the distance. I remembered there was a vacant field. I squinted, trying to penetrate the gloom. Gradually the greenish glow resolved into a row of shimmering figures floating in a haze and gliding above the ground seemingly without effort. The figures moved horizontally from right to left, as the sounds of the roaring train continued. A steam whistle hooted, and a pitiful moan of human pain drifted across the field.

"It's the Ghost Train!" I wailed. "The old man at the tomb predicted it."

Toby was having none of that. "Ghosts, my ass. It's some jokers putting on a show, trying to scare us."

"They're doing a good job of it."

"Those aren't ghosts. They're men. I'm going to get a closer look."

"Ghosts or men, they're not friendly to us. Leave them alone."

"I'll be careful. They'll be expecting us to come out the front. I'll use the back door and go around the house. Stay here." Before I could stop him, Toby had grabbed a jacket and slipped out the back. Bending low, he kept the jacket over his head as he made his way toward the apparition in the misty field. In seconds, he had disappeared into the night.

A light flicked on in Mom and Dad's cottage. They had been awakened by the noise too. I quickly pulled on jeans and a sweatshirt and left by the back door. I scurried across the parking area to join Mom and Dad, banging on their patio door and calling out that it was me. Angie—apparently she was sleeping in tonight—let me into the living room. She pulled at my sweatshirt, like a child desperate for attention. "It's the Ghost Train, just like Brian said! That means there's going to be another death." I tried calming her down and explained Toby's view that the whole thing was a hoax. Dad appeared in his pj's just as I was saying that Toby had gone out to confront the pranksters.

"This could be trouble," said Dad. "I'm going out to help him." He started for the bedroom to get his clothes.

"Jim, you stay right where you are," Mom commanded. "We don't need both of you in danger."

"Toby knows how to take care of himself," I said. "But I'll go after him just to make sure he's okay. You better stay inside, Dad."

"Then take this," said my father, handing me a baton-sized flashlight, suitable for double duty. "And don't do anything foolish."

"I won't. No, don't turn on the front light. That way they won't be able to see me leave." I slipped across the darkened threshold and stole across the parking area in front of the house. I headed in the direction of the greenish haze. But within a dozen paces, the mist congealed into fog, and the green light disappeared. The flashlight proved useless when I aimed it toward the ground. The beam reflected the opaque surface of the fog, creating a cottony glare. A moment later I stumbled over a clump of grass and went sprawling, and the flashlight flew from my hand. I patted the ground around me until I found it, then resumed my forward progress. I remembered the hedge only when I reached it. Exploring with an outstretched hand, I probed for an opening. I found a break eventually and pushed through it, into the field where the apparition had appeared.

The sounds of a train had faded away. I pushed on, looking for some sign of Toby. I was afraid to call his name, fearing that I might attract the unwanted attention of a ghost or a rascal. Suddenly my fear was realized: a lumbering shape emerged from the fog. The figure bore the outline of a man but had a pale, unearthly mien. Its face and groping, outstretched hands were no human color but a ghastly green, and in an instant my rational mind deserted me. I reverted to instinct and screamed, confronted as I was by a ghoulish spirit from beyond the grave. The creature rushed directly at me. I threw up my hand to ward off the charge, but that defense was ineffective. My palm slid across a clammy green cheek, and I hit the ground hard.

The next thing I knew, my head was cradled in Toby's lap and he was stroking my forehead. "You're bleeding," he said. "How do you feel?"

"Fit as a broken fiddle." It was meant to be a game reply, but lame was more like it. Gingerly, I rose to my feet. I tested them and was pleased to find they still worked, in a fashion. I looked around for the flashlight, but it was lost.

"Easy," he said. "You took a bad tumble."

"Toby, one of those things attacked me, and it wasn't human. I saw it up close. It was green."

"Uh-huh. Like your hand?"

I raised the appendage in question and was shocked to see a green palm glowing in the dark. "What the . . . ?"

"Phosphorous paint," said Toby. "You must have brushed some off the guy who knocked you down. Makes you glow green in the dark. When I was a kid we got hold of a can of it one Halloween and scared the hell out of the neighborhood."

"So they weren't ghosts after all?" He shook his head. "But what about the train we heard? It sounded like it was right outside the cottage."

"It probably was. Some joker playing a track of sound effects."

"But I saw them too, the people sitting in a row, looking like they were on a moving train."

"They were parading behind a hedge about waist-high, so you couldn't see the lower half of their bodies. The fog and your imagination did the rest."

"But why go to all that trouble?"

"To scare us off. Get back at the family of the developer. And have their fun. C'mon. Show's over. It's damp out here, and that cut needs cleaning."

I don't like being fussed over. Thank God, Toby didn't try to commiserate while he was fetching bandages. Mom's not a gusher either, but she's mom enough to wince when she sees her child bleed. So we made a stop at our place to wash the scrape on my forehead. It wasn't bad, but the head bleeds worse than other places, so I applied the offered Band-Aid. Then I fluffed my bangs so they hid the spot, and we went next door.

Dad opened the door before we knocked. He had been on alert since we left. How long had we been out there—five minutes, fifteen, more? Whatever it was, it was too long for my family. Dad hugged me to his chest. Mom grabbed Toby with one hand while she reached for me with the other. Pretty soon we were in a group hug, with Angie looking on.

Four o'clock in the morning is the reverse of teatime, but tea is what an Irish family does if they don't do whiskey. The story took longer to tell than to happen, what with Angie's excitement, Mom's worries, and Dad's practical questions. Like good reporters, we gave them a clear picture of the what and the where. But the who and the why were as foggy as the night. Someone wanted to frighten us, but why? To make us leave the island quickly? What good would that do, and for whom? Dad thought the escapade must have to do with his brother's death: Bert's killer got his friends to give us the spooks so that we would take off for the States. The guards would send Bert's body back home, give up on a weak case, and leave Bert's killer free.

Toby was looking up the way you do when you're trying to remember something. "What are you thinking?" I asked.

"That crowd yesterday at the butcher's shop. Some of them might do something like this."

Mom spoke, and I froze. I saw the witch face emerging. "I'm not surprised," she said, looking at Dad through squinting eyes. "Bert's tearing this island apart, even from the grave. This railway project is just one more of his selfish, rotten schemes. The man held nothing sacred—not nature, not community, not family." Tears were welling in her eyes, but she was not breaking down. She was still fierce. "What a legacy!"

Dad rose and took his cup to the sink. His back was to me, so I couldn't see his expression, and I didn't need to. He was bereft, and Mom was making it worse. Maybe Dad wasn't thinking that. Maybe it was just me. Thankfully, while I sat at the table thinking bad thoughts, Toby took the teacups to Dad and helped him wash up, while Angie took Mom's hand and led her to bed.

12

EVEN TEA-SOAKED, the Barnes family sleeps like hounds before a hearth, but Toby was jagged by the caffeine. He sent me to bed, while he stayed up reading, in the kitchen. The better to hear any further pranksters, he said. When I came seeking breakfast four hours later, he was still at the table, with a satisfied smile.

"What's up?" I asked.

"Ah, the question is, What's under?" He reached under the table and pulled up a muddy boom box. "Haven't seen one of these in a while, have you?" he asked.

"I had one in my dorm. Where did you find it?"

"On the other side of the hedge, where you saw the green ghosts. I went out at dawn, just in case I'd find anything they left behind—a hat or a coat. And there it was, a boom box with a CD in the slot, and here's what it plays."

He pressed a button, and a whistle split the air. My hands flew to my ears, and he turned the volume down. The whistle gave way to metal wheels squealing against iron tracks, as the steam engine propelled its train forward.

"There you have it," said Toby, punching the off button. "The ghost train rides again!"

"Clever devils," I said. "How did they get hold of train sounds like that?"

"They could get any sound effect off the internet, and you'd think they would have played it from a phone or a tablet. That would have been risky, though. If they dropped a device like that, we could trace who they were. Someone went to the trouble of burning a CD from their sound source."

I remembered Angie's role in the upcoming play. "There's a theater group here," I told him. "Someone must do their sound effects."

"Sure. Let's ask Bobby about who's in the group and whether they have a boom box."

"First thing after Fruit Loops," I replied. I was starved.

"Fruit Loops and coffee coming up. You need a kick start."

The sight of Toby stirring instant espresso powder into a mug of hot water put me well off coffee. "I'll stick to that excuse for orange juice in the waxed carton," I said.

He put the coffee mug in front of me anyway. "Frank Hickey just called to remind us we're invited to tea this afternoon to see the Paul Henry painting, the one Bert bought for their railway poster. You said you wanted to see it. Still interested?"

"I am. What time?"

"We're due at his place at three. But if you don't mind my saying so, you look a wreck. Drink up."

That gave me the jolt I needed. Here was the chance to kill a flock of birds with one stone. I could see an important Paul Henry painting up close, one that had never been shown to the public. For the sake of Aunt Laura and Emily (now half owners), I could assess its value if they were to resell it here in Ireland, where it would fetch a better price than in the States. And most important, while we were visiting, Toby and I could size up Frank himself. What exactly was his stake in Bert's railway project? Did he stand to gain from Bert's death, or to lose? I wanted to know.

After washing mud off his hands, Toby brought me the tourist map and pointed to the south side of the island. "He lives way down here in this village at the tip. Derreens. Looks touristic."

What Toby meant was that there were multiple symbols on the tourist map marking its location: a pyramid with a cross on it (meaning a church), two lines of crosses (a historical cemetery), a castle turret, a boat, fish, and a sprinkle of dots (a sandy beach). I knew the spot. Derreens was near Kildownet Church, where Maggie had taken me. I hadn't noticed a village, but among the map's touristic symbols were the letters P.O., so there were enough living residents to warrant a post office. I had seen the dead residents already at the ruined church.

"On the way, I can show you Kildownet graveyard, where they buried the bodies from the disasters. It's beginning to look like the killer is connected to the train project—maybe one of the environmentalists who want to stop it, or a descendant of one of the families involved in the tragedies."

"Does that mean you've stopped worrying that your mom is guilty?"

"It means that if I could find evidence pointing to someone else, I could stop worrying. So far it's all speculation."

I asked Toby to drive so I could navigate. Both my memory and the map said that the turnoff from the main road was just before the town hall at Achill Sound. I looked for a sign for Derreens, or the Atlantic Drive, or the pirate queen's castle, or Kildownet Church. But if the sign existed, we missed it. We turned around for a second try, and this time we saw a low panel displaying the symbols for water, church, and castle. The words were in Irish and looked unrelated to our destinations, but the symbols were promising.

When we turned, I recognized the pink rhododendrons, the yellow gorse, and the flatlands beyond. This territory was different from our side of the island. Here there was a strong sense of isolation. You tended to see only one house at a time, hugging the road for safety or daring to roost near the water, surrounded by acres of scrub grass. The land wasn't farmed, and we saw no cattle, but I spotted a rundown bar at the corner of a lane. A handmade sign indicated the way to Derreens. As far as I could see, there was no town in that direction, only the dry slope of an unnamed mountain.

The sight of the familiar ruined church, roofless and open to the sky at the side of the waters, was heartening, a sign of human community, past and present. Toby pulled over and parked on a grassy strip by the side of the road. There was no real place to park, but since we were the only visitors, that wasn't a problem. We got out and crossed the road. A light breeze stirred the grass.

"Let's see the graves first," said Toby. "Then we can do the church." He swung the creaking gate, which scraped across its stone base. I led him to the right of the church and showed him the stony Famine plot. We stood for a long while, gazing at the ground containing countless starved bodies. I was thinking of my ancestors and what they must have suffered in those horrid times.

Shaking off that disaster, I led Toby to the other. We stepped over sunken spots and, taking care not to step on recessed gravestones, we crossed behind the church and wended our way among small and large headstones from a jumble of periods—the 1950s, the 1920s, then some from the 1800s. We stopped now and then to read the names and inscriptions, when they were decipherable. We came finally to a communal plot segregated from the other graves by a low iron fence. I saw again that its iron bars created a square of grass that might have been a park, if it weren't for the fact that dozens of skeletons lay beneath the ground. In the back of the square, on the side by the water, rose the tall monument topped by an Irish cross. Under the cross was a request to passersby: "Of your charity, pray for the souls of"—and then came the names of thirty-two young people who, as it said on the base of the monument, "were accidentally drowned in Clew Bay on June 14th 1894."

Between Maggie and my reading, I had pieced together the story of the tragedy. Because the island was so poor, its young men and women used to work in Britain in the summers as seasonal farm laborers. Those buried here were bound for Scotland to work in the potato fields. Several hundred workers boarded four boats on June 14, 1894, departing from Darby's Point on the south end of the island. They were sailing only a short distance to Westport on the mainland, where they would transfer to a large steamship for Scotland. But the small boats were overloaded, and trouble struck as they neared the harbor, where the steamship was waiting for them. Many of the youngsters had never seen a ship that size, and to get a better look, they crowded to one side of their boat, shifting the load and causing the boat to capsize. The thirty-two who drowned ranged in age from twelve to forty. To the small community of Achill, it was a devastating loss.

"Imagine losing your son like that," Toby said. "Or your daughter. Half of these are girls' names." He paused, to read more. "And half the girls are Marys. Look. One family lost four children—the Cooneys. The O'Haras lost three."

"And they all came home in coffins on the Westport-Achill rail line," I said. It must have doubled the horror when people remembered the old prophecy that one day iron carriages would come to the island spitting smoke and fire and carrying death.

Toby asked, "How did it happen that it was the train's first trip?"

"At the time of the drowning, the line had been completed but it hadn't opened yet," I explained. "It was pressed into service early to bring the bodies home."

Toby shook his head in dismay. "Then what happened on the last train run?"

"That was in 1937. A fire in a dormitory in Scotland killed ten boys from Achill who had gone there to pick potatoes. They brought the bodies home on the last train to Achill before the line closed. How eerie is that? You can say it was just coincidence, but no wonder people believed the prophecy had come true."

Toby was staring at the monument. He pointed to a name. "The three O'Hara girls, for instance. Sisters, maybe. Think of the parents waiting at the new train station to claim the bodies. The whole island probably turned out for the funeral. And the telling of what happened would come down through the generations. You can see how the islanders wouldn't want their tragedy used to make money."

"You're thinking of Michael O'Hara, aren't you?" I asked.

"He started that bar fight over this, and he was one of the leaders at the protest yesterday," Toby pointed out. "He's got a hot temper."

"And a motive for wanting my uncle dead and out of the way."

"Correct, although there are others on the island who had the same motive."

We stood in silence, contemplating the scene. I pictured the crowd gathered around the plot on the day of interment. I wondered what the weather was that day. For us, the sun shone, sparkling on the water at the edge of the graveyard's slope. A pair of cawing gulls dipped and turned out over the channel. Old headstones leaned this way and that. "Come on, let's go see the church," Toby said.

He reached the ruin before I did. I was calling out something about getting on our way to Frank Hickey's so we wouldn't be late when I heard Toby say, "No!" In a moment I saw the reason why. We weren't late. Frank Hickey was. He was laid out at the foot of the stone altar, his blank eyes looking up but blind to the sky. I thought of the old man at the megalithic tomb; he had prophesied another death, and here was the corpse of Frank Hickey. Toby knelt and checked for a pulse, then shook his head.

"Better not touch anything," I said, though at first I saw nothing at the scene that suggested violence. There was no blood or any injury to the body except a scratch on the left cheek. I pointed to it and said, "Toby, what do you make of that little scrape?"

He leaned over the body and peered at the cheek. "I guess it could have happened if he fell against the altar. Or somebody could have hit him."

"Could a bare fist leave that kind of mark?"

Toby looked again. "Something with a sharp edge might. A ring maybe."

"A claddagh ring?"

"Yeah, that would do it." Toby got to his feet. "We better call the guards."

13

WE DROVE TO THE MAINLAND, following a garda vehicle. The second murder on the little island merited investigation higher up the chain, at Westport Garda Station. The square, stucco building wasn't very inviting, but then again, what jailhouse is? It didn't help that we were ushered in through the back door.

Sergeant Flynn unsmilingly explained that back-door entry was a courtesy, so we wouldn't be seen by the general public. Small comfort, that. Flynn handed me off to a female guard and took Toby down the hall. I was left in a small room, painted an unnerving yellow. I suppose the sunny walls were meant to make up for the lack of natural light, as there were no windows. The room didn't even have a two-way mirror, the kind you see on detective shows. But then I noticed a wall-mounted video camera, which was already on. I could see my image in the monitor next to the camera. My lips were pressed thin with tension. My frown made me look hostile. Would I trust somebody with that nasty face?

It was a long time until Detective Inspector O'Donnell arrived. He offered me a cup of tea, which I declined. His mug was in his hand. He plunked it on the table and sat opposite me. He dunked a biscuit, fumbled as it crumbled on the way to his mouth, salvaged a bite, and dusted the crumbs from his lap. He slumped back and folded his arms. "You know, suspicious deaths on Achill are a rarity. Yet you discovered a body the day after you arrived. Here it is, less than a week later, and you've come across another one. Now, I ask you, what are the odds of that?"

"I know how it looks, but I'm telling the truth," I insisted. "We stepped into the church and saw him lying there. Are you saying I'm a suspect?"

"I didn't say you were a suspect. You're here voluntarily, to make a statement, since you discovered the body."

"Then why am I being recorded?" I pointed to the camera.

"For future reference. It's routine. Perhaps you can tell me why you were at Kildownet this afternoon."

"Frank Hickey had invited us to his house for tea, and Kildownet was on the way, so we stopped to see it. I'd been there once before and wanted to show my husband the monument for the Clew Bay drownings."

He rocked back on his chair and stretched out his long legs, crossing them at the ankles. "You say you were invited for tea. If Mr. Hickey expected you at his home, what do you suppose he was doing at Kildownet Church?"

"I don't know, Inspector. He might have been there in the morning when he was . . . when whatever happened to him happened."

"You were going to say 'when he was killed'?"

"I suppose so. All I know is that my uncle was murdered and Frank was his partner. There was ill will toward both of them on the island, as I'm sure you're aware. So, yes, my first thought was that he was killed. Have you determined the cause of death?"

"Not yet," said the inspector. "The autopsy will provide that information." He looked at me for a long moment before continuing. "How well did you know this man? You say he invited you for tea."

"We met twice, once at my aunt's house and once at the Annexe Bar, but I hardly knew him. The reason he invited us over was to see a painting he and my uncle owned. I told him I'd like to see it."

"Oh? What painting is that?"

"A landscape of Achill Island by Paul Henry that they planned to use for a poster to promote their steam train and hotel."

"How valuable a painting are we talking about?"

"I haven't seen it, but it could be worth a substantial sum."

"Give me an idea."

"Two hundred thousand euros, maybe more. If you need a professional evaluation, you might ask Declan O'Leary. He's a Dublin art dealer who has a summer home here."

"I know who he is," said the inspector. "How do you know him?"

"A friend introduced us. Paul Henry came up in the conversation. He mentioned he wanted to buy that painting himself, but my uncle outbid him for it at auction."

This information interested O'Donnell. He wrote something on the pad next to his mug. "How did Mr. O'Leary take that? Was he bitter about losing the painting?"

I hadn't meant to compromise Maggie's ex, but the inspector had a point. Declan might be willing to kill to get his hands on a painting that meant a great deal to him. I pushed aside the thought and shrugged.

"Where is it now, the painting?" asked O'Donnell. "Is it in Mr. Hickey's house?"

"I assume so. We were asked there to see it."

Inspector O'Donnell continued scribbling notes.

I was having second thoughts about mentioning Declan's name to the inspector. "Don't you think there are far more likely suspects?" I asked. "Frank Hickey and my uncle had real enemies here, all those people who want to preserve the greenway and prevent the railway project."

"Are you thinking of anyone in particular?"

I described the attempt last night to frighten us with fake ghosts. "And then there are the descendants of the Achill tragedies who might have their own reasons to want the project stopped, Michael O'Hara for instance." I mentioned the fight he had provoked with Frank at the Annexe Bar over dishonoring the dead.

"I'm well aware of the protests," said O'Donnell. "Garda Mullen has an eye on the leaders. We're working closely with him." The inspector tilted his chair back on two legs again and asked, "Can you suggest any other person who had a reason to attack Frank Hickey?"

The image of Bobby Colman's claddagh ring flashed through my mind. The mark on Frank's cheek could have been caused by such a ring, but Bobby had no reason to harm Frank that I knew of, and besides he seemed to me a sweet guy. Not to mention that Angie was gaga over him. So I replied, "No."

I felt my strength ebbing and wanted to end this if I could. "You said my presence here today was voluntary. If that still holds, may I be excused?"

"You're free to go if you wish. We'll draw up a statement on the basis of what you've said. Come by tomorrow to review and sign it."

I meant to walk away with the nonchalant glide of the innocent, but I don't think I succeeded.

14

I'M ONE OF THOSE DELAYED-REACTION PEOPLE—dry-eyed at the funeral but bawling in the car, weeks later. Five days out from finding Bert's body and hours after finding Frank Hickey's, I finally had the shudders. Toby got me home, held me tight, and insisted I nap. When he woke me, I was in mid-dream, fighting with Mom to stop her from immolating herself, like the Buddhist monks in Tibet. Eyes open, I felt an awful throbbing in my chest as Toby said something unintelligible. Then I understood. He was giving me a choice. Did I want to cancel our evening plans or pull myself together and go? "Remember?" he said. "We're having dinner with Maggie and Declan."

I checked my stomach and found it calm. I could make it to dinner, so long as nobody made me eat.

We were meeting in Dugort at Masterson's Pub, where the windows face west to the sea. We drove there on the same road I had walked with Dad, but there were no sheep this time. It seemed a harder drive than our walk had been, because of white light reflecting off the water. Even sunglasses at eight in the evening didn't kill the glare. At the pub, I tried to snag a seat turned away from the sun, but I didn't succeed. Though our friends hadn't arrived, Declan had reserved the best table for sunset, right in front of the picture window. The table was U shaped, so that everyone could have a view. The best I could do was to sit on one end and angle myself toward the room. It was a large space, not entirely filled with tables. In the back, a noisy group of men were playing darts. The house was full, though, with families feasting on fish and chips.

I ordered ginger ale for my queasy stomach, and Toby predictably asked for Guinness. While we waited, he told me how he had spent the hours I had slept through. He had gone over to Mom and Dad's to tell them about our discovery of Frank's body and our interviews in Westport.

"I wish you'd told me. I should have gone to Mom and Dad before I took the nap. All this is making me muddleheaded."

"Don't worry," Toby said. "Your folks decided to visit Laura to tell her about Frank. They didn't want her hearing it on the news."

That was a novel picture, Mom comforting Laura.

Our drinks arrived at the same time as our friends, and there was a bustle at the table. Maggie had Happy on a leash, but he wrapped himself and the leash around the waiter's feet. Maggie dropped the leash, untangled the waiter, and took Happy by the collar, the better to dress him down, while Declan stood back, wincing. The experienced waiter kept the tray level, served our drinks, and went off to fetch wine for Declan and Maggie.

She begged us to forgive Happy. He was just a pup, eight months old, away from home, and of a feisty breed.

"Dogs have to be trained," Declan huffed.

"People have to be patient," Maggie countered. "Look at him now, good as gold." He was indeed curled at her feet, looking at the floor in submission.

Declan sniffed to express his displeasure.

Toby began talking about Frank's death before I had a chance to warn him off. In my opinion, it wasn't a good idea to give Declan too much information before the inspector got to him, but Toby didn't seem to have that concern. He took the story step by step, and when he got to our discovery of the body, Declan pounced. "Do the guards think it was murder?" he asked.

I sensed it was time for me to roll things back. "All we saw was the body. The guards cleared us out fast, so we don't know."

"You must have given a statement," he said, with a note of protest.

"We each did," Toby said. "They questioned us separately."

Maggie leaned in with such interest that Happy rose up, wanting part of the action. With one hand, Maggie batted him down.

Undeterred, Declan threw out a barrage of questions, but Maggie intervened. "They already told you they don't know anything. They found the body, that's all." There was more hostility in her voice than the situation warranted, and I sensed they had been spatting on the way over.

Supper was served, and I ate a buttered roll. For the whole meal, Declan and Maggie were at each other. After a while, I dropped out of the conversation. Toby didn't seem to pick up on the couple's discord, but he did notice I had withdrawn. He looked around for the waiter. "I know it's early," he said, "but I'm going to take Nora home. It's been a hard day. You can see she's beat."

"I'm all right," I protested. "We can stay a while."

Maggie settled the matter neatly. "Why don't you boys go over there and throw some darts?" she said, cocking her thumb to the back of the room. "The girls want a chat."

"That's our release," Declan said. "Come away." Toby shrugged and followed Declan to the dartboard.

Maggie waved the waiter over and got him in a huddle. "Would you send those fellas two pints of Gat?" she said, pointing to the banished pair. "Then we'll be ordering dessert if you'll bring us a menu. And a bowl of water for the dog, if you don't mind. Grand."

"You're asserting your dominion over dogs and men," I said.

"Staying in the same house with that man, I have to. He's driving me mental. Everything has to be done just so, his way. I can't even boil an egg without getting corrected. I'm getting fed up."

"So, Declan's not a threat to your Thierry?" I liked Maggie's French boyfriend. Though Maggie was considerably older than Thierry, they seemed a good match.

"Lord, no! I miss his beautiful young body, not to mention his courtly ways. The boy knows how to treat a woman." She went on shamelessly detailing their romantic life, in and out of bed. It was far more enjoyable to talk about sex than death. Before long, her patter about one appetite whetted another and I began to crave that dessert, so I ordered Irish apple cake with custard sauce. Maggie went continental with tiramisu and prosecco. When her glass was empty, she slapped it on the table. Happy sat up expectantly, inquiring with his snout on his mistress's knee whether it was time to go. She patted him back down and he resumed his subordinate position.

Smiling slyly, she said, "Remember that swingers' club we talked about? Declan told me they're on for tomorrow night." She paused and looked me in the eye. "Guess what? We're going."

"You're going to a swingers' party with Declan?"

"Not with Declan, darlin'. With you."

Through a mouth of apple cake, I sputtered my objection. I meant to give a clear no, but it came out more like ni, ni, ni, ni, choke. Maggie patted me on the back, handed me her napkin, and continued undeterred.

"We'll have no trouble getting in. They're always looking for attractive women, and aren't we gorgeous?"

"Getting in isn't the issue. The issue is what kind of trouble we'll get into, once we get in. I'm happily married, Maggie. Monogamy is my middle name."

"Haven't you and Toby ever talked about experimenting a little?"

"To tell you the truth, he's been pestering me about that club from the moment he heard about it, but I've been putting him off. We're perfectly happy as we are, just the two of us."

"Well, then, you're lucky. I'm not asking you to break your vows. I'd just like to get in there and see what it's like. I missed my chance, donkey's years ago. Now's the time."

"Fine," I said. "Carpe diem. But carp without me."

"The thing is, Nora, I'm not brave enough to go on my own. If I have to defend myself from a Celtic satyr, I want a pal to help me out." When I looked doubtful, she admitted, "If I find a satyr I like, I'll make a date with him for later."

It was fine for Maggie. She would sate her curiosity and maybe find herself an Achill man. What was in it for me? The sight of more pale skin than a Dublin dermatologist sees in a month? "Maggie," I said. "Look around you. Would you like to see this crowd naked and rutting on the floor?"

Maggie surveyed the scene. "It might be interesting," she said. Then, wrinkling her nose, she added, "At least in some cases." I wasn't convinced. She assured me that everyone would be clothed, at least at first. "There's a disco. And I hear there's a nice spa. You can wrap yourself in an ample towel and just watch."

"I still say, no thanks." You would think that with me sober and Maggie half-sloshed I would be able to hold my own. Maggie, however, had an enticement up her sleeve.

"If you're keen to know what happened to Frank Hickey, or your uncle for that matter, you couldn't find a better place for snooping. There's more gossip in that club than there's shells on the shore. Frank Hickey was a member, and people will be talking about his death. What with the music and the dancing and the liquor, folks loosen up. They let it all hang out. Literally."

I couldn't help laughing, and Maggie noted the breach in my dam. I parried weakly: "If I'm going to do this, and I'm not saying I will, Toby has to come. It's a swingers' club. People will arrive in couples before they mix it up, right?"

"On the whole, yes. They need extra women, though."

"Why?"

"You Yanks *are* naïve, aren't you? Use your imagination."

"If I do, I'll have to wash it out with soap."

Maggie sighed. "We promise nothing by walking in the door. We'll be welcome because we're single women. Men have to be vetted by the members. They don't let them just wander in off the street, and they have to pay a fee. But women get in for free. If we go together, we'll be fine."

"How am I going to sell that to Toby?"

"You're not. Don't tell him."

"I can't do that. He'd be furious when he found out."

"He doesn't have to find out. It'll be our little secret. Well?"

I bought time by taking a sip of water. Some women may fantasize about sex with a lot of partners, but I'm not one of them. My hormones are focused on one randy man. I've never considered a swingers' club, with or without my randy man. Now that I had the opportunity, though, I confess I was a mite curious. The prospect of picking up rumors about the murders was a lure, and on that basis I was leaning toward going. Besides, I would have Maggie along as guide and protector. But not telling Toby didn't sit right.

We were ready to go, but the men were still at the back, surrounded by spectators, male and female. We split the bill and went to join the group, where we found Toby, who had been eliminated in an early round. Declan now was matched against Michael O'Hara, the hothead who had picked a fight at the Annexe pub. O'Hara was wearing a red flannel shirt that matched the color of his face. He had had a lot to drink, and his general appearance was disheveled. Food crumbs clung to the flannel of his shirt, the remnants of a slovenly meal. As he drew his hand back to launch his dart, I noticed that he was sporting a claddagh ring, which led my thoughts back to the cut on Frank Hickey's cheek. Of course, Bobby Colman had a similar ring and, for all I knew, so did half the men on the island.

The spectators were all on O'Hara's side, and I recognized a few faces from the demonstration. They were calling out encouragements. "Knock him out, Michael!" "Kill him!" "You can get him on the double-six!" I knew nothing about darts, beyond that hitting the board is good and a bull's-eye is better. I assumed Maggie knew more. I asked, "Why are they telling him to go for the six? Shouldn't he aim for the center? That's marked fifty."

"You're right for ordinary darts," Maggie explained, "but this is a game called Killer. You start with several players. The first goal is to become a 'killer.' You need five points for that. Then you can knock out other players. It's complicated. It's enough to know that Declan was assigned the number six, and his opponent will knock him out if he gets his dart into the double-six. That's it over on the right, there."

"If the guy knocks Declan out, he's the killer?"

Maggie shook her head, smiling at my ignorance. "No, they're both killers already. But he'd be the winner."

I didn't get it, but I pretended to. Declan took his position and swung his wrist back and forth, envisioning the precise arc that the sharp dart would fly. Without warning, he shot the dart into a number just left of the bull's-eye.

"Triple-eight," Declan called. He was smirking.

O'Hara spat on the floor but offered his hand to his opponent. Declan shook it with the haughtiness of a military victor; the man was nothing if not competitive. I could imagine his irritation when Bert outbid him at auction. It must have galled him to learn that the painting he wanted was now in Frank Hickey's possession. Would Declan kill to obtain it? He was a killer at darts, but that's not the same thing.

I slept badly that night, disturbed by nightmares. I recall only fragments: a room full of naked people throwing darts at me because I was wearing clothes; a body laid out on a dining room table. Then I was trapped under a rock and couldn't get out until a strange little man lifted the stone and pulled me up. He kept making the universal sign for hunger, repeatedly bringing the tips of his fingers to his mouth. I woke to find myself cradled in Toby's arms. It was dead black in the room. "Shush," he soothed me. I must have called out in my sleep. For the next several hours, I teetered on the threshold between sleeping and waking until a weak gray light hit the curtains. Suddenly, I snapped awake and sat up, with the knowledge of who killed Frank Hickey and how it was done.

15

CRUMBS CLINGING TO A FLANNEL SHIRT from forcing a loaf of crumbly brown bread down the victim's throat. Asphyxiation, leaving no marks on the body except a small cut on the cheek that could have been made by a claddagh ring. The signs pointed to Michael O'Hara.

Excited, I shook Toby awake and shared my solution. "Death by soda bread," he scoffed. "It's hard to believe. Besides, a dream isn't evidence." He pursed his lips and raised a finger. "Yet there *is* a way of testing your theory. If you're right about how Frank was killed, the autopsy will show an unusual amount of bread in his stomach."

"But what if he had digested the loaf by the time they did the autopsy?" I protested. "That's what happened with the landlord who was choked, according to the old man at the tomb."

"There's where the legend has a flaw in it," Toby reasoned. "When you die, the digestive process comes to a halt. That's why a coroner can tell what the victim's last meal was by examining the contents of his stomach. But I've got another idea," he continued. "Tell them to do a test of O'Hara's ring to see if there are any traces of Frank's DNA on it. If O'Hara clipped him on the cheek, the ring would show evidence of it."

Thanks to Toby, I could propose scientific methods to confirm my hunch, which gave me the confidence to share my theory with Inspector O'Donnell. It was too early to call right then, but an hour later I reached the Westport station and was put through to O'Donnell at his home. I laid out my hypothesis, and he was responsive. As soon as the autopsy results were available, he would check the analysis of the victim's stomach contents, as well as his mouth and throat. I also relayed Toby's suggestion of performing lab tests on O'Hara's ring. "Let's see what the autopsy shows first," said the inspector, "before jumping to conclusions." He quizzed me carefully about my observation of the crumbs sticking to O'Hara's shirt. Even as I was answering, I worried that O'Hara could have cleaned his shirt or trashed it. Without physical evidence, my testimony would be weak. But all this was hypothetical for now. The inspector thanked me and reminded us to stop by the station later to sign our witness statements. Maybe he would have news then about the autopsy.

It was still early morning, and I had offered to make breakfast for Mom and Dad. Toby encouraged me to go, saying he would make something for himself. I hadn't mentioned the swingers' club yet. I needed more time to sort out how I felt about Maggie's idea.

I took eggs and milk from the fridge and filched the bread too. (Toby would be reduced to dry cereal.) With these ingredients in my arms, I walked awkwardly to Mom's door and let myself in. She was at the kitchen counter, frowning as she measured ground coffee. Pale skin and squinting eyes aged her, as did the slump of her shoulders.

"How about I make you your favorite breakfast?" I asked.

"You mean *your* favorite breakfast," she replied, once she had glimpsed my cargo.

"Come on, you eat it up like chocolate."

"That's because it's you making the breakfast," she said, straightening up. "It's been a long time." Her eyes softened.

She was thinking, I suppose, of the years after Angie's birth, when I became the family cook. Mornings, from middle school through high school, I made French toast for Eddie and me. And I always made extra, so that after we had gone to school, Mom could have a quiet breakfast. Lukewarm, but quiet.

On Achill, I didn't have my secret ingredient, a teaspoon of vanilla, but Mom had some cinnamon that previous tenants had left in the cupboard. In a square baking tin, I whipped up the cinnamon, eggs, and milk, added a pinch of island salt, and sneaked in an unorthodox dash of sugar. Then I put two slices of bread in the pan to soak up the good goop. Funny, I thought, how many uses there were for an Irish loaf. Then, while frying the soaked bread in sweet Irish butter, I told Mom about my interrogation. I felt the trust between us returning as we compared our interviews, hers at Achill station, mine at Westport. We had felt the same anger and fear. At that moment, I chose to believe in Mom, that she was innocent.

Dad and Angie followed their noses into the kitchen, and together we did in the loaf of bread, six brown eggs, and all the milk I had brought. Feeling closer after our feast, we began the day that had long been planned. Toby and Dad were going off to sample "some of the best sea angling in Europe" (as touted by the island's website). Dad had invited Mom; she was the more experienced angler. As a girl, she worked the lines on her father's fishing boat, and she still has a passion for the sea. This time she declined, with the excuse that Toby and Dad needed "guy time." "Meanwhile," she said, "the Barnes women are going on a tour of the coast towns, in search of artisanal wares." That was the old Mom, proposing adventures and games.

Keel is Achill's hub for the sale of arts and crafts, so that's where we headed. We parked in the lot at Keel Strand, and were drawn onto the sand to watch a few minutes of a parasailing class. The setting struck us silent: a deep white beach curving for miles along a bay bookended by mountains. The sky had been graying since morning, and it was swept by milky clouds. The beach was empty except for a few figures at the water's edge. They must have been coaches for the fledgling followers of Icarus. On the water, bright sails fluttered, as wet-suited bodies struggled to fight waves and wind. The effect was bracing.

When we turned away toward the shops, our hair whipped in our faces. Mom laughed as Angie threw herself into a well-executed cartwheel. It felt like the old days, when we were a family in Rockport, by another shore of the Atlantic. My eyes stung, from the wind maybe, but also from a sense of difference. Then we were young, anticipating joys to come. Now we carried with us the memory of death, and worry for each other in the coming days.

I don't know what Angie felt, but she acted in high spirits, taking us from this shop to that, encouraging purchases. She led by example, buying a present for her convent: a white altar cloth embroidered with Celtic crosses. Without her prodding, I would have passed up a gallery of bogwood sculptures. What a depressing name, I thought. But I found them bewitching, redolent of Achill earth, carved from wood preserved for thousands of years in peat. I selected an arching dolphin, who would link my memories of Achill to my hometown, Rockport, where dolphins have always played, as well as to my current home, Bodega Bay, where dolphins have recently arrived.

At every gallery, Mom took photos of displays. She was getting ideas for her tourist shop back in Rockport. When the kids were young, Mom worked there part-time, for fun and money. But when Angie went to middle school, Mom got career-serious and made it to manager. Before Angie was a sophomore Mom owned the shop, employed her two best friends, and was proud of it.

Since the Beehive sold tourist items from key chains to crystal, Mom wanted to compare its wares with those in her shop. It was after one o'clock, and the logical thing was to lunch there. I would have to forget the last time I visited the Beehive, when I had examined the sweaters for buttons like Mom's. I didn't quite succeed in putting it out of my mind, but lunch was good—a hot fish chowder, suited to the cool day. We talked about friends in Rockport, Grammy's illness, and my brother's coming baby. Nothing about Bert or murder.

Mom wanted to start in on the crafts and trinkets, and the Beehive had three rooms of them. I stayed behind to pay the bill. I didn't see Angie or Mom in my first walk through the salesrooms, but I found them on the second pass, in the back of the last room, in front of a full-length mirror. Angie had her hands on Mom's shoulders, adjusting the fall of a hip-length sweater.

Spotting me, Angie said, "This looks great, don't you think?"

I couldn't disagree. The close-knit wool glowed green, with blue low-lights, becoming tones for anyone, and splendid on Mom. The cut was stylish, a far cry from the lumpy mass of the sweater with the missing button. I checked the buttons on this one. There weren't any. The fabric fell in an open drape from a softly rolled collar.

"No buttons," I said. "Will that be warm enough for winter?"

"Sure it will," Angie said. "She can pull it close, like this."

"That won't be as warm as your blue sweater," I warned. I had come around to look Mom in the eye, but she gazed at herself, in the mirror.

"I'm sick of that old thing," she said, still not looking toward me. "It's ready for the dustbin. Besides, the buttons are falling off. I've already lost one and the others are loose."

My ribs knit. It looked as if Mom meant to get rid of the blue sweater, now sitting at the cottage with one missing button. Was that because she feared the button would be found near where Uncle Bert was murdered? I tried to work out her plan. She could dispose of the old sweater, but where? Maybe she had done so already.

"That's too bad," said Angie. "Did you lose it here?"

"Somewhere on the trip," Mom replied in an offhand manner. "Do you really like this on me?" She looked at herself sideways in the mirror.

"I do," Angie said.

"I'll take it," said Mom, setting her jaw decisively.

For me the day's bright moments darkened.

16

BY EVENING, I HAD MADE UP MY MIND about the swingers' club, but I hadn't yet told Toby. He was tired from a day of fishing and welcomed the idea of an evening at home while Maggie and I took a girls' night out. When he asked where we were going, I couldn't hold it back.

"To that swingers' club you're always talking about," I said.

"Very funny."

"No, it's true, but it's not what you think."

"Wait just a minute." Toby sprang up from the couch. "You mean to tell me that my happily married wife of seven years—"

"Eight."

"Eight. But I got the happily married part right, didn't I?"

"Absolutely. Deliriously happy."

"Good. Let me start over. So my deliriously happy wife of eight years is planning to sneak off to the swingers' club without me?" Toby had his palms extended out, like a picture of St. Francis talking to the birds.

"I'm not sneaking off. I'm pre-confessing, right now. Let me explain." I sat him down and related everything that Maggie had told me about the club, stressing the possibility of picking up a clue about the murders, through loose talk. "Think of it as undercover work," I said.

"Sounds more like 'no cover' work to me," Toby snapped.

I tried to address his concerns. According to Maggie, we could spend the evening as spectators rather than participants, so long as we looked ready for action. She didn't specify what that meant. Wrapped in a towel? Stripped to the skin? Clad in black leather and carrying a whip?

"Why can't I come too?" Toby asked.

I explained the entrance policy that excluded men who weren't members. "Don't worry. Maggie's going with me. She'll have my back."

"I'm worried about who'll have your front," said Toby. Now that he was wisecracking, I knew I was making progress. It's Toby's way of overcoming discomfort. We talked the idea through, and he finally relented. "But I want a full report," he warned. "No touching. And no looking, just listening."

"I don't know about the looking clause," I said, "but I'll do my best."

"And keep your phone with you at all times," Toby insisted. "That way you can call me if you get into a tight spot. I'll be right outside, waiting in the car."

Having a getaway car at the ready seemed smart, but how was I supposed to carry a phone? If you're naked, do you hold it behind your back? Maybe I could grab a towel and twist the phone into it.

When Maggie arrived, she wasn't pleased to learn that Toby was coming, but he promised her he would stay out of sight and avoid spoiling her evening. "Just don't crash the party," Maggie cautioned, "or we'll be booted out."

"Understood," Toby replied. "But I'll be there if you need me." Having agreed on the ground rules, we set out in Maggie's car, with me in the passenger seat (left side) and Toby head-down on the back seat, in fetal position.

The Achill Arms—or as Maggie calls it, the Arms & Legs—stands on the Dugort road on the outskirts of the village, where the beach gives way to a high spit of meadow. The wide, two-story building sits at the center of this meadow, with its back to the sea and its face shielded from view by a high wall of fuchsia. In summer, the shrubs are thick with red and purple flowers, sparing passersby from any glimpse of shenanigans inside. The hotel's heyday was the 1920s, but when train service to Achill ended, tourism dropped off and the island's grandest hotel went into decline. It was abandoned by midcentury and stood empty for decades, until a publican from Keel bought it at auction rates and renovated it for use as a private club. One wing of the hotel was turned into a spa with a communal hot tub, a hickory-paneled sauna, and a steam bath lined with Italian tile. The other wing, which once housed a restaurant, was transformed into a disco with a stage, dance floor, and discreet nooks. Upstairs, of course, were the bedrooms.

It was just getting dark when we arrived. We parked at the end of a line of cars and prepared to leave Toby in the back of Maggie's Toyota with the windows rolled down. He had his backlit Kindle to keep him occupied, but it was not going to be pleasant lying scrunched up on the cloth seat covered with dog hairs. Just before I closed the car door, Toby raised his head to whisper, "Remember!" He pantomimed a phone call, with his pinky extended and thumb to his ear.

"Will Declan be here tonight?" I asked as we walked up the path to the hotel.

"I doubt it," Maggie said. "He spent the day at the garda station and came back exhausted. It seems the Paul Henry painting was missing when the guards searched Frank Hickey's house. Declan claims he doesn't know anything about it, but the detectives questioned him for hours. It's just as well he won't be here," she added.

At the entrance, we rang the bell and waited. "How do I look?" I did a slow turn. I had spent some time wondering what to wear.

Maggie nodded her approval. "You look like someone going to an orgy."

My suitcase hadn't carried hussy clothes to Ireland, so I was reduced to adapting my one sexy nightgown, which I had brought to encourage vacation romance (with my own husband). It was a wedding-shower gift from my girlfriends, who had splurged at Victoria's Secret on a black knee-length number, which fell in slinky folds from string straps. I added fake gold earrings and the real gold necklace that Toby's mother gave me as an engagement present. To solve the phone problem, I slung the strap of a black purse across my chest, thereby accentuating my best bits while housing my escape alarm.

When I saw Maggie's getup, I realized that I had gone too far. She was in tight jeans and a white V neck T-shirt. Wild red hair said all that needed to be said.

The door was answered by an unnervingly handsome man in a white silk shirt and black leather vest. Greeting us with a slight bow, he said, "Good evening, ladies. I don't believe I've had the pleasure of seeing you at the club before. How did you find us?"

Maggie brushed by him. "One of the members invited us." She mentioned Declan's name. "And we were interested," she said, smiling salaciously.

"Ah. I don't believe he's here tonight. But you're very welcome." He returned Maggie's smile. He had unnaturally white teeth. "May I take your wraps?"

While he was hanging up our coats, Maggie whispered that she wouldn't mind wrapping herself around our genial host. Maggie could use a little more impulse control.

The host returned, his Cheshire cat smile intact. "My name is Sean," he said, as if offering us (or rather, Maggie) his calling card. "I'll be happy to show you around the club and go over our rules—we don't have many, but they have to be observed."

"Grand," said Maggie.

"Right, then. Well, you may have noticed that I didn't mention my surname when I introduced myself. Here it's first names only: that's rule one. And you are?

"Maggie."

"Nora."

"Right. You'll get on fine. Rule two: all acts of intimacy are consensual. If someone approaches you and you're not interested, just say so. Here 'no' means 'no.' This rule protects our guests from unwanted contact."

"That's brilliant," said Maggie.

As long as everyone observes the rule, I thought.

"Rule three." Sean ticked off on his fingers. "Dress code. Clothing is optional throughout the club, but our guests in the bar and disco are usually dressed. At the spa, nudity is the norm. There is also a shower area and locker room, where you may leave your belongings."

"Do you provide towels?" I asked.

"Of course."

Just checking.

"And upstairs?" Maggie inquired.

"Upstairs pretty much anything goes," said Sean. "It's up to you. One more thing," he added. "To protect everyone's privacy, no photographic or recording devices are allowed. You have to check your mobiles at the door." He extended his palm.

Uh-oh. So much for my communication link with Toby. If I got groped by a masher, I was on my own. Maggie and I fished in our bags for the phones and turned them over.

"Thanks, ladies," he said. Sean stowed them in a box containing other phones, each with a numbered label attached. "You can claim them on the way out. Your number is fifty-eight, remember that. Now if you come this way, I'll give you a quick tour."

We were standing in the entrance to the old hotel. Sean led us into what once had been the lobby, now converted to a stylish bar, with dim lighting, a curved wooden bar, and café tables. "It's the ice-breaker room," he said. "Most of our guests like to start out here with a drink. I recommend the Cooley 2 Gingers." Whatever that was. I looked over at several couples and a group of four men, fully clothed, sipping drinks and exchanging conversation. It could have been any hotel bar in Ireland.

We followed Sean into a room across the hallway. "Things start to warm up in the disco," he said in a raised voice. The room was basically dark but lit in flashes by strobe lights and a pulsing chandelier. Recorded music pounded, singles and couples danced frenetically, and hips bumped suggestively.

Sean led us out. "At the end of the hall," he continued, "we have the spa: hot tub, steam bath, sauna, and locker rooms." I noticed the plural. At least there would be a women's changing room.

The spa had slate floors, warmed by mellow lighting. Yup, everyone was nude, though a few women and a single bashful male had wrapped themselves in spa towels. The focus of activity was a huge hot tub, packed with chattering bathers, not a swimming suit among them. Other guests lounged on recliners, the kind you see at a pool. An area at the back of the room was marked off for badminton. Two well-nourished couples were batting a shuttlecock over a net, flopping and bouncing as they scurried after it. The scene reminded me of Bosch's *Garden of Earthly Delights*. "This is more like it," Maggie said.

We've all seen naked people before, but a room full of them is something else. Here there were all shapes and sizes, some young, some middle-aged. With their clothes on, most of these folks would be unremarkable, but here they turned heads, displaying parts more interesting than those normally in view.

"The women's locker room is through here." Sean pointed, indicating a door. "The bedrooms are upstairs. I'll leave it to you to find them, when you're ready." His job done, Sean bowed again and returned to his post.

"I wonder if we were supposed to tip him?" Maggie said. "You know, like a maître d'?"

"Could be."

"No matter. We can take care of that on the way out. So, where to first?"

"Let's get a preview of the second floor so we'll know what's what," I said, "and then go to the bar. I'm not ready for the hot tub, and the disco's too noisy."

"Right," she said. "Em, what's the plan if we get separated?"

"Separated?" Maggie looked at me impatiently until I got it. "Oh. Well, what time does this place close?" I didn't relish the idea of being left on my own, but why should I spoil her party?

Maggie said, "I'm not sure, but pubs close at twelve thirty on Saturday night."

"Then let's meet at the bar at half past eleven. I don't want Toby to have to sit in the car all night. Will that give you enough time to, er?"

"It will if I get lucky. Lead on."

The upstairs bedrooms still had the look of a hotel and hadn't required much renovation, except that the interior walls of some of the rooms had been knocked down to provide larger spaces for cavorting. A few rooms had glass doors, catering to any voyeurs in the corridor and exhibitionists inside. "Over here," Maggie summoned me. "This looks like the main event." In a big room at the end of the hall the beds had been replaced by gray mats on the floor. The mats gave the impression of a gymnastics match or yoga class. Various combinations of men and women were going at it, but it seemed to me there was more effort involved than fun—they were all too busy concentrating on their performances. I pictured a row of judges holding up number cards.

"I think I get the idea," I said. "I'm ready to go down to the bar."

"Lead on," said Maggie.

The bar had filled up while we were touring the club, but we were able to get a small table at the back. Maggie got up to fetch our drinks and returned with a whiskey for herself and white wine for me. In her wake came a pair of lads carrying drinks of their own.

"Hiya," said Larry, introducing himself and pulling up a chair. "May I?" he asked after the fact.

"Why don't you take a seat?" said Maggie pointedly.

"Beg pardon" said Larry, getting up.

"No need," said Maggie. "I was just codding you. You're welcome, and your friend too."

"That's Jonathan," he said, breaking into a broad smile. Jonathan said hi and sat down opposite me. Larry was freckled and on the roly-poly side. His friend Jonathan was better looking but shy: the drag-along.

"So, girls," Larry began, "what brings you to the Achill Arms?"

"Just visiting," I said.

"Just visiting, eh? Well, what do you say we get the visit started." He winked. "Which is it to be, the hot tub or upstairs?"

Maggie intervened protectively. "D'ye fancy a dance first, Larry? How about the disco?"

"Delighted." Larry had focused his attention on me, but now that he had a bird in the hand, he adjusted his sights. Off they went, leaving me with tongue-tied Jonathan. The next ten minutes were painful reminders of my junior high school prom. Eventually I disentangled myself, announcing an unneeded trip to "the ladies.'" I hoped to find a source of information elsewhere in the building.

Thinking the spa might be worth a go, I disrobed in the women's locker room and emerged in a fluffy spa towel that did a pretty good job of preserving my modesty. I spotted unoccupied lounge chairs on the far side of the hot tub and chose one, doing my best to appear at ease. It wasn't long before two young men claimed the chairs next to me. The skinny one had a towel around his waist, while the well-built one strutted, swinging his towel provocatively. The friends spread their towels over the chairs, casually exposing themselves, and stretched out. I pretended to doze while I eavesdropped on their conversation.

It was pretty distasteful stag talk, but my eyes popped open when one of them mentioned Frank Hickey. I sat up, tucking my towel under my arms. "Excuse me, do you know Frank?" I asked.

"I do," replied the muscle man. He gave me the once-over. "Did you hear he's just died, God bless him?"

"Yes, I heard," I said.

"Terrible thing," he went on. "I was just talking to him the other day. The club won't be the same without him."

"What happened?" asked the skinny guy, sitting up and swinging his legs over the chair.

"They're not saying," replied the first, "but I'd lay ye five that it's . . ." He stopped himself and said to me, "Was Frank a friend of yours, then?"

"We were some kind of cousins, many times removed."

"I wouldn't speak ill of the dead, you know, but odds are someone did him in. Frank wasn't content to keep it at the club. He tomcatted all over the island, so plenty of husbands were ill set toward him. No offense," he added, looking at me. "But that's how it was."

I shrugged and said, "I hardly knew him."

"Wasn't he running around with Betty O'Shea?" asked the skinny one.

"Sure, that was common knowledge."

"And Bryan O'Shea has a black temper. He nearly destroyed Keene's Pub last year."

"He's a bad egg, that one, but he's not the only one wanting to bust Frank's dial. Our man was sneaking behind the back of that American partner of his who turned up dead."

"Bert Barnes?" My voice came out squeaky.

"That's the one. You'd never guess the wife would go for a fella like Frank, but isn't that the way sometimes with the quiet ones? There's a story there, and it will come out, I'll tell ya."

"Is that right?" I asked, struggling to sound only mildly interested.

"He told me so himself. You'd think he'd be satisfied with the goods here at the club, but some men can't help courting trouble."

"Speaking of which," said his friend, ogling me, "Can I interest you, my dear, in a visit upstairs?"

"No, thank you. I'm not quite ready for that," I replied.

"How about the hot tub, then?"

"I'll come too," said the bodybuilder, with the implication that his offer should close the deal.

"You guys go ahead. I'd like to relax here a little while longer, if you don't mind. I might join you later."

"It's a date," said one.

"See you there," said the other.

They left, leaving me to recline with my eyes closed, thinking about Aunt Laura and Frank Hickey. My mind went back to the condolence call on the morning of Uncle Bert's death. The front door was closed, but Frank came into the house without knocking or ringing the bell. That suggested he was used to coming and going. If Frank and Aunt Laura were having an affair, what implications did that have for Uncle Bert's death? Did Bert try to have it out with Frank and get killed in the bargain? Or did Aunt Laura use Frank to rid herself of Bert? Maybe she hated Bert more than Mom did. Now that was an unsettling thought.

I sat up on the recliner and took another shock. A man who looked awfully familiar was entering the steam bath. Toby! I would know that backside anywhere. What was he doing inside the club, prancing around buck naked? He was supposed to be out in the car. I bounded up, almost losing my towel, and circled around the hot tub to the steam bath. I pulled open the door and looked in, but the room was opaque with billowing steam.

"Don't stand there with the door open. You're letting out the steam," boomed a male voice, not Toby's. "If you're coming in, come in. And lose the towel."

I stepped forward, pulling the towel up under my arms, and closed the door behind me. "Toby?" I asked.

"I'm Ryan," said the voice. "Have a seat."

"Join the party," said a female voice. "I'm Sheila."

"Glad to meet you," I said in a faltering tone. "I'm Nora. I was looking for my husband."

"Why?" asked Sheila. "You can have him at home. What's the point of coming to the club?"

I peered through the steam and could make out, just barely, two naked figures sitting side by side, Ryan and Sheila I presumed. I made bold to call out, "Is anyone else in here?"

"No," croaked a low voice from a corner of the impenetrable fog. That scared me out of my—well, I was already out of my clothes. I tightened the towel around me.

"Toby, is that you?" I asked. I felt like Winnie-the-Pooh calling into the rabbit hole, X-rated version.

"Ribbit," the voice croaked.

"Sorry to bother you," I replied. Backing out the door might make me look like a prude, but I had no intention of staying and meeting the croaker. That weirdo couldn't be Toby; I must have been mistaken. It was too bad my phone had been confiscated, because now would be the time to use it.

I retreated to my safe haven on the recliner, but no sooner had I made myself comfortable than I faced another difficulty. Larry and Jonathan had entered the spa. I pulled the towel up over my face, hoping the guys hadn't spotted me yet. I didn't want to extend the acquaintance that Maggie began in the bar, but where to escape? The steam bath was out. The hot tub was unthinkable. The locker room was too far away. My best option was the sauna, a few feet behind me.

I pivoted and stepped inside, the towel still shielding my face. A blast of hot, dry air almost sent me back out again—that and the realization that I wasn't alone. A man was sitting in the corner with a towel draped around his neck and everything else exposed. He was big, bald, and hairy. Uh-oh, I thought.

"Hello there," he greeted me. "I'm Simon."

I gave my name and sat on the bench opposite. I intended to watch his every move.

"You're going to be hot in that heavy towel," he observed.

"I'm fine as I am," I replied.

Nothing more was said for some time. The heat burned through my skin and melted my muscles, or that's how it felt. Just when I thought my bones were softening, Simon the Bald crossed over and sat next to me, *very* next to me. "Why don't you take that off," he coaxed. "You'll enjoy it more."

I clenched the towel to my chest and edged my rear down the bench. He put his hand on my knee. I took it off. "No, thank you," I said. "I'm not interested." He persisted. "No means no," I said. "It's a club rule."

"Is that so?" he said, trying to slide his hand up my thigh.

I shoved him away, and my towel came off in his grip. "That's better," he said, tossing it aside and leering at me. He had me squeezed into a corner, and I was scared.

"Get off," I cried.

"Or what?" he said, pawing me. "I know what you want." He mushed his face into mine.

Just then, the door to the sauna flew open and Toby, wearing only a scowl, launched himself at my attacker, prying him off me and slamming him into the wall. As Simon bounced off, Toby seized him by his shoulders and forced him into a sitting position on the bench. "That's my wife," said Toby, standing over him. "Leave her alone."

"How was I to know?" sputtered Simon. "Besides, what's she doing here if she doesn't want to play?"

Toby ignored him. "Come on," he said to me, grabbing my towel. "Put this on and let's get out of here." Toby put his arm around my shoulder and guided me toward the locker room.

"Boy, am I ever glad to see you," I said, stumbling a little. "How did you get into the club?"

"There's a back door. Declan told me about it when we were playing darts. I took my clothes off and left them in the back hall, behind a chair. I don't think anyone saw me."

I explained why I hadn't been able to use my phone.

"I realized something was wrong when I called and you didn't answer. Where's Maggie?"

I told him we had agreed to rendezvous in the bar at eleven thirty.

"Okay, we'll wait for her," said Toby. "You get your clothes on. I'll get my stuff and change in the men's locker room. Then we'll meet in the bar. I'll be the guy in crinkled clothes."

Over drinks, still shaken from my ordeal in the sauna, I told Toby what I had heard about Frank Hickey.

"Well, that gives us a new lead. If your aunt was involved with Frank, we've got a whole new set of possibilities. Where there's a triangle, there's trouble, every time." Toby took a long draught of his beer. "I have to hand it to you. Your gambit of sleuthing in the nude has paid off."

"I don't know if it was worth almost getting raped," I admitted. "It's a lucky thing you came along when you did."

"It wasn't just luck," said Toby, putting down his pint. "I planned to sneak in all along. You don't really think I'd let you loose in a swingers' club by yourself, do you? I kept tabs on you from the start."

"So that *was* you I saw going into the steam room. I thought I recognized your rear!"

"Sorry, but I went upstairs first, in case things had gone too far for my comfort. When you weren't in the den of iniquity, I came down to the spa. You weren't in the hot tub, so I opened the door of the sauna, and there you were, battling with that hairy beast."

"You're sure you weren't in the steam room before that?"

"Nope. I don't like wet heat."

"That's strange. Some weirdo—never mind. I was just glad to see you when I did. You saved my ass."

"Truer words were never spoken," said Toby.

At eleven thirty, Maggie sashayed into the bar, looking pleased with herself. While she sipped a nightcap, I gave her a rundown of my evening, omitting the incident in the sauna, then asked about hers. "Just grand," she replied. She had spent most of the time upstairs.

"With Larry?" I asked.

"Get on with you. I ditched him at the disco."

"Who then?"

"No last names, remember?" And that was all I could get out of her. We reclaimed our coats and phones. Maggie tipped the host. She winked at him too. We got in the car, and damned if she didn't hum all the way home.

I went to bed exhausted, yet feeling amorous. Perhaps it was a delayed reaction to the sight of so many naked men prowling for partners. Or maybe it was the sight of my own preferred partner, standing by our bed, naked and at the ready. I drew him to me, and we made love passionately, then tenderly.

Later, drifting off to sleep, folded against his body spoon-style, feeling blissfully content, I whispered, "Good night, sweetheart."

"Ribbit," croaked Toby.

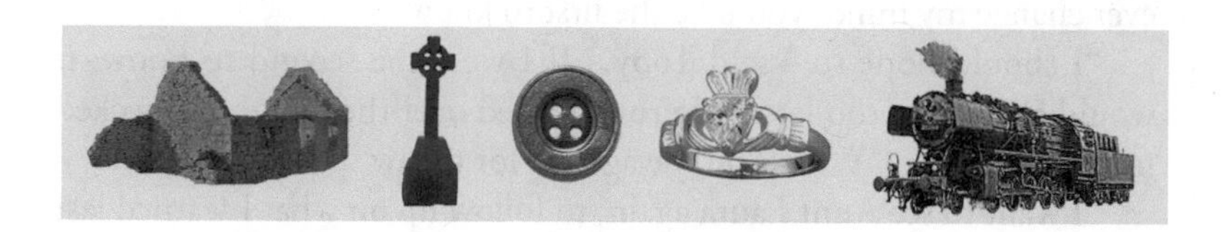

17

YOU IDIOT. I knew it was you."

"You mean, the toad in the steam bath?"

"Who else would pull a stunt like that?"

Toby grinned and spread some marmalade on his toast. The rain, which had held off for most of the week, had come down heavily during the night. Outside it was gray and everything was dripping.

"So, tell me what you thought of the club," Toby pursued. He took a sip of his coffee. "Would you go to one again, just for fun?"

"By myself?"

"Don't be ridiculous." He knew I was teasing.

"With you?"

"Of course with me."

I reflected for a moment. "Well, seeing you naked in a roomful of your peers was educational." I paused. "You held up pretty well."

"Gee, thanks."

"But if you're thinking of adding swinging to our repertoire, forget it. I'm not excited about sharing you—or being shared."

Toby actually looked relieved.

"And I'd never consider going by myself. Tell you what, though. If I ever change my mind, you'll be the first to know."

"I should hope so," said Toby. "If I were the second to know, it would already be too late." He rose, leaned over the table, and pecked me on the cheek. "What's on the agenda for today?"

"I want to see Aunt Laura again, to follow up on what I learned last night. But I think it's best if I go by myself. What do you think?" Toby nodded, waved, and went off to his shower, leaving me to do the dishes.

While cleaning up, I considered what I had learned at the Achill Arms. Island gossip said that Laura and Frank Hickey were lovers, and I could believe it. Frank wasn't my idea of a match, but he was attractive. Anyone could see that. Nonetheless, at this point the affair was only gossip. What's more, an affair didn't prove that Laura and Frank had conspired to murder Bert. Still, I had to pursue every possibility in hopes of exonerating Mom.

It was too early to call on Laura, so I decided to stop at the Deserted Village on the way. If there was no one supervising the crime scene, I would mount the hill and take a look. I wanted to remember exactly how Bert lay within the ruined cottage.

As I approached the village, my eyes went to the tented ruin, standing white and geometric, surrounded by the remains of other houses, half-destroyed by weather and time. I tramped up the hill, over wet grass, losing my resolve with each step. I was loath to confront the memory of Bert's body.

In the end, the site gave me no data. The officials had tented the scene so thoroughly that I couldn't make out what I had come to see: the size of the room where Bert had fallen, how close his body was to each wall, how much room the killer would have needed to fell Bert with a blow to the head.

Yet that moment did give me something. My mind made a projection screen of the white sheet before me. I saw Frank Hickey standing at Bert's back, raising a ragged rock and crashing it onto his partner's head.

That was completely plausible. I imagined Laura sitting at home, erect on her couch, with hands folded, waiting for word that the evil deed had been done. Though it didn't come as naturally, I tried to transform the picture so that it featured Laura, rawboned Laura, bringing the rock down on her husband's skull. I realized she wasn't tall enough to have hit him while he stood. He would have to be bent over or already knocked to the ground. But it could have been done, perhaps by herself alone or perhaps with Frank's assistance.

What about Declan O'Leary? Yes, I could picture him killing Bert with a stone, but it seemed a stretch to believe that he would murder Frank just to obtain a painting.

As for Michael O'Hara or one of his crew, there would be no trouble downing the older and less active man. One stroke, and the environmentalists would have had their victory.

But Mom? She was a healthy woman, with the sort of strength built by housework and moving boxes at the store. I had to admit she was stronger than Laura, as well as several inches taller. She might be as fit as Frank Hickey, for that matter. But I couldn't imagine her striking anyone from behind. She would confront her opponent face to face, I was sure.

That was all I could glean from my stop at the Deserted Village, so I picked my way down the slippery hill and followed the lane to my aunt's door. She was the one who answered my knock. Her ravaged face hinted that she was grieving over two men. I scotched my prepared script and took a few minutes to take off my muddy shoes and talk about the rain. That done, I offered condolences regarding her husband's partner. The graciousness of Laura's response surprised me. She offered me tea and took me to the kitchen to make it. There was no false ceremony, just the homely movements of two women brewing a cuppa with tea bags in mugs. I carried the mugs into the living room, and she brought a plate of store-bought cookies. We were set up for a talk, not an interrogation. I thought I had better let her lead the way.

"You and Toby are the ones who found Frank, I heard," she said in a hoarse voice.

That was my cue to tell the story, omitting ugly details and softening the rest. She knew less about our discovery of Frank's body than I expected, but that made sense. She wasn't next of kin—the officials wouldn't have felt obliged to give her the details.

"He was a lovely man," she said wistfully, with her eyes cast down. The tension in her face relaxed, as if those simple words gave her solace. She spoke of Frank warmly, and she hadn't spoken of her husband at all. That said something.

I watched her pick up her mug in both hands, as if to steady herself. She looked up and said, "Thank you for coming, Nora. Your parents were here last night. You've been so kind, all of you. After all these wasted years." She said she was sorry that our families had become estranged. As a consequence, Emily hadn't had Angie and me as friends while she was growing up. Seeing Emily alone in her sorrow, with her cousins so close to hand, made Laura realize what her daughter had missed. It hardly seemed to me that Laura was at fault here, and I said so. As far as I could tell, it was Bert who had alienated our family.

"I could have set it right," she protested. "I never questioned Bert's version of things."

I waited for her to explain, but she stayed silent, shaking her head, with eyes half-closed. To cover for the awkward moment, I stood up and went to the window, hoping to find something to say about the front garden or the weather. With a remark in mind, I turned back toward Laura, and my eye caught something gold behind the antique cupboard by the window. The edge of a frame, I guessed. I couldn't help asking about it. "Aunt Laura, is that a picture frame behind the cupboard?"

Her lashes fluttered and she leaned back slightly before saying, "Yes, actually. I've put it there for safekeeping."

I remembered the last time I had heard that phrase. It was in connection with a valuable painting by Paul Henry. "I'd love to see it. May I pull it out? I'll be careful." I had my hand on the frame before she could reply.

It was wedged in more tightly than it should have been for safekeeping. I had to get my hand in under the bottom of the frame and support it while I moved it around until I found the exact position from which to retrieve it safely. Then there it was, the painting I had seen on Frank's phone. It was a wonderful work. The photo hadn't conveyed the subtle tones of the mist-bleached sky, nor the variegations of green and purple in the mountains rising from the waters of a still, slate bay. The realism of that natural background differed stylistically from the impressionist strokes that rendered thatched cottages in the foreground. Yet some artistic force held the elements in tension. There was no mistaking Paul Henry's unique touch.

So while the guards were questioning Declan O'Leary about the painting, it was here in Aunt Laura's house, more or less hidden in plain sight.

Laura broke the silence. "Emily bought that, last year, for the hotel."

"Oh? I heard that Uncle Bert bought it, at an auction in Dublin."

She sniffed. "He probably did the bidding. He was good at that sort of thing, you know—bluffing and pouncing—but it was Emily who found the painting."

I carried it over to Laura and placed it on a chair, so we both could see it.

"It's beautiful," I said. "Was it hung in this room?"

"It was in Bert's study, but when we went home for the winter he asked Frank to hold it. The islanders know the value of a Paul Henry. Why tempt them to robbery?"

That was pretty much what Frank had said, but it didn't explain how the painting had ended up here. I gave a warning: "The gardai are looking for it and they think it might be connected with Frank's death."

"If you're thinking I killed Frank to get that painting, it's the last thing I'd do. Frank was my only friend on the island."

I decided to be blunt. "He was more than a friend, wasn't he?"

Laura looked at the floor and then at me. She sighed. "And what if he was?" She held my glance and spoke matter-of-factly, with no hint of embarrassment. "We were both taken in by Bert, and it was a way to get even with him. So, yes, he was more than a friend. I suppose that will all come out now. But it wasn't a serious relationship. Frank had other women, and I knew that."

The direct manner in which she admitted the affair suggested she was telling the truth. If so, there was no great ardor on either Frank's side or hers. So much for my "crime of passion" theory.

"Frank was a friend," she continued, "but family comes first. I wanted the painting for Emily, and I was afraid he wouldn't give it up."

"How could he refuse? It belonged to Bert and Emily, didn't it? They bought it."

"In the name of the syndicate. God knows what else is tied up in the name of the syndicate. But that's another story. The painting is one item I could secure for us, for Emily." As she spoke her daughter's name, her voice softened, but it hardened again as she continued. "There's a legal battle ahead, about who owns what and who owes what. Well, possession's nine-tenths of the law. I wanted that painting in our house, not in Frank's."

"But when did you take the painting? We were on the way to see it at Frank's house when we found his body."

"If I'd known you were going to visit him, I'd have stayed away. I knew that Frank was going to Kildownet that morning, to look at the mass graves. He had this idea that if we did something to honor the dead who were brought home on the death trains it would win goodwill for the project. But we couldn't just duplicate the memorials at the graveyard, so he wanted to take photos of what's there, and that's what he was doing that morning. I drove to his house quite early and parked beyond his drive, so I could see when he left. I was in and out quickly."

If that was true, it meant that Laura had an alibi for Frank's death. She was at his house to take the painting while he was at Kildownet struggling for his life. She looked at the painting and then made a dismissive wave. "Put it back where it was," she said.

While I carefully slid the painting into its tight slot, she added, "Keep this to yourself, Nora. I want to take the painting with me when we bring Bert's body home. For Emily. You understand."

"I understand, but you need to tell the guards that you have it. They think it's been stolen and they're questioning people about it." I thought of Declan going through a grilling. "It would be better to tell them you have the painting than for them to find it here."

"I suppose you're right. I'm so tired I'm not thinking straight." She leaned back and closed her eyes. For the next few minutes we sat in

"Our tech team discovered fibers at the crime scene that we are trying to match with articles of clothing," explained O'Donnell. "They were found on Mr. Barnes's body but didn't come from any of the things he was wearing, so they must have come from someone who came into contact with him." He lifted a plastic evidence bag and displayed it by walking around the table and then approaching Mom and me. "There are several different fibers," he continued, shaking the bag gently. "Cotton, rayon, and wool. They come from different articles of clothing, and they may have come from more than one person. Or not." He addressed his last comment to my mother. "So, if you don't mind, we'd like to have a quick look through your closets and bureaus to check for any item of clothing that could be of interest."

"And what if we do mind?" asked Dad.

"I'm afraid it's not up to you, sir," said Sergeant Flynn, tapping a folded document on his hand.

"They have a warrant," Toby repeated.

"It's best if you cooperate," said the sergeant. "We'll try to be careful and leave things as we found them." He and O'Donnell pulled on thin latex gloves.

"Go right ahead, then," Mom said, with a shrug. "We have nothing to hide. Angie, how about a pot of tea while these officers do their work?"

Angie got up and set about making the tea while the detectives went off to the bedrooms. Heat washed over me, and I pulled at my sweater's sleeves, to cool myself off. Fibers, I muttered to myself. If Mom had lost a button from her sweater at the scene, it was more than likely a thread had come off too. Now the detectives had recovered the thread, and it was only a matter of time until they matched it with her sweater. My effort to shield Mom by concealing the button had been in vain. I could feel my heart pumping me into a panic. My eyes darted around the room and met Toby's. He glanced nervously at my parents' bedroom door. Mom, however, seemed confident and calm as she went about setting the table for tea. From Angie's room, we heard the sounds of bureau drawers opening and closing. About a quarter of an hour passed.

"Nothing here," announced the sergeant as he emerged from Angie's room and crossed the hallway to my parents' bedroom, where the inspector was doing the search. Dad looked sour. Toby feigned indifference. Angie and Mom fussed with the tea. And I stared at the floor, trying to hide my anxious thoughts. The last time I had seen the sweater, it was hanging on a hook inside the door of my parents' bathroom. Mom hadn't worn it since. Had she gotten rid of it? That was a possibility. Or maybe it was hanging in her closet or folded in a drawer. I listened to the sounds of rifling from the bedroom. I hoped she *had* gotten rid of it. Then it occurred to me that Mom's sweater wasn't the only item of clothing that could implicate her. According to O'Donnell, multiple fibers had been found at the crime scene, not only wool threads. What if fibers from a different article of Mom's clothes could be matched with those in the evidence bag? She must have been wearing a blouse under her sweater and probably cotton pants. It wasn't just the matter of a button; she was in double, maybe triple jeopardy. My heart sank as my belief that she was innocent and someone else guilty slipped away.

Mom poured the tea. I stirred an extra sugar into mine. Dad asked, "Where have you been all day?"

"At Laura's," Mom replied, which was partly true.

"You missed a call from Sister Bridget," Dad told us. Bridget had been at a week-long retreat following her Jubilee celebration and had just learned of the events on Achill Island. "She's coming up tomorrow to be with the family."

"It will be good to see her," said Angie. "It's too bad she can't come today. She'll miss my performance tonight." The production of *The Playboy of the Western World*, in which Angie had a minor part, was scheduled for that evening. We all were going. Despite the death of Uncle Bert, we were determined to root for her.

"I expect she'll be a help to us," said Dad.

I thought so too. "Where will she stay?"

"At a B&B in Keel," said Dad. "It's run by one of her friends."

Sister Bridget had friends all over the island. We were here because of her recommendation—unlucky though it had proven to be.

We sipped our tea quietly. The only sounds were the clinks of spoons on saucers.

"All right, we're done here," announced Inspector O'Donnell from the hall to the bedrooms. As an afterthought he added, "Sergeant, will you show Mrs. Barnes what you found?"

"Aye," came the reply. Sergeant Flynn emerged, carrying one of Mom's old pullovers—it wasn't the cardigan with the missing button but a different sweater. I didn't know whether to be relieved or alarmed. "I don't think this is going to be a match a-tall," he said as if to reassure us, "but we'll just take it with us and run a few tests. I'll write you a receipt and you'll have it back soon enough."

"This is ridiculous!" Dad stood up from the table.

Mom forestalled him. "You do what you have to, Sergeant. I guess I can get by without it for a day."

"Thanks for your cooperation, missus," he said, folding the sweater into a large plastic evidence bag. "Sorry for the inconvenience." They made ready to leave. Well, I said to myself, they still don't know about the missing button. And Mom doesn't seem at all disturbed about the pullover. So that's good.

Then the inspector said, "May I have a brief word with you?" motioning me to step outside.

Now what? He followed me out the door.

"It's about Michael O'Hara. It looks like you were on to something when you spotted those bread crumbs on his shirt. The pathologist confirmed an undigested mass of soda bread in Frank Hickey's esophagus. He could well have been asphyxiated by someone forcing bread down his throat, and O'Hara's a likely suspect. The thing is, he did a runner when we came to arrest him. Like as not, he was tipped off. Word travels quickly on this island. And if that's the case, O'Hara could be aware that you're the primary witness against him, so have a care. He's at large and dangerous. We'll find him all right, but until we do, keep an eye out and give us a call if you catch sight of him, will you? Here's my mobile number, in case you've misplaced it."

The inspector handed me his card. I nodded. As they got into their cars and left, my nodding turned into general shaking. I was scared as hell. Toby, who had come outside at the sound of the departing cars, folded me in his arms and patted my back. I felt like a baby being burped—and that thought shook me back to adulthood. We agreed not to tell Mom and Dad about the warning, to keep them from worrying about me.

Back inside, Mom was attempting to placate Dad, who still had his dander up about the house search. She reminded him that we were all going to the play tonight to support Angie and that we should try to get into the right frame of mind to enjoy the show. A little later, Bobby Colman came by to pick up Angie for the final run-through. Mom announced she would take a nap before dinner. Dad went too. Toby and I returned to our cottage, and while he read, I slept fitfully on the couch. I woke with an ache in my jaw. I must have been clenching my teeth.

18

IT HAD STARTED RAINING AGAIN. Driving across the island to Achill Sound, Toby made an effort to sound upbeat. He had read up on *The Playboy of the Western World* and was trying to prime us for the production. "It's about this nerdy guy who becomes a celebrity by telling a tall tale," he explained to Mom and Dad, who were sitting in the back. "He shows up in this backwater where nothing ever happens and tells the locals the police are after him for killing his father with a spade. The kid expects the villagers to turn him in, but instead they hang on every word and the girls start following him around like a rock star."

"Angie plays one of them," I added. The windshield wipers slapped back and forth, making a sound like someone beating a rug.

"I don't get it," said Dad. "Don't they think he's done anything wrong?"

"That's the question," Toby allowed. "When the play opened in Dublin the audience was shocked. In fact, there was a riot in the theater.

But Synge based the play on a real event. It happened here on Achill in the 1890s. A man named Lynchehaun attacked an Englishwoman who owned the estate he was working on. She tried to evict him, and he wouldn't have it—burned down her house and beat her so badly that she never appeared in public again without wearing a veil to cover her face. He was convicted of attempted murder, but he escaped and made it to America. While he was on the run, the people of Achill hid him and fed him, and he became a legend."

I asked, "Why would they help a brutal man like that?"

"For one thing, Lynchehaun was a local man and the landlady was English," Toby answered. "Another is that he made fools of the police. The islanders built him up into a daring criminal who'd defied the law."

"Even though it was attempted murder?" asked Dad.

"I know," said Toby. "Anyhow, Synge followed the case and turned it into comedy. I won't say more because I don't want to spoil the play for you. It's full of surprises."

"Hmm," said Dad, still skeptical.

"Well," said Mom. "I hope it all goes well for Angie."

The Achill Sound town hall, tucked behind a miniature strip mall at the entrance to Achill Sound, had been converted to a theater for the occasion. At one end of the hall a temporary wooden stage with curtains had been erected. Rows of folding chairs provided seating for the audience, and there was a small bar at the rear of the hall for refreshments during intermission. The bar was a permanent installation. Whatever use the hall was being put to, the islanders always could enjoy a pint.

Even though we had arrived early, the place was packed. It seemed the whole island had turned out for the production. I spotted Aunt Laura and Emily two rows ahead of us on the aisle. We waved and settled in behind them. An usher was handing out folded programs. Mom eagerly opened hers and scanned the cast of characters. Bobby Colman, playing Christy Mahon, the lead, was listed at the top, and in last place at the bottom was our Angie, billed as one of the village girls. "Look," Mom nudged Dad, "Angie's name is on the program. Isn't that a kick?" Dad said "Hmm" again, but this time it meant he was impressed.

Right on time, at 8:00 p.m., the lights in the hall dimmed and the curtains opened, revealing the set: the interior of a rundown pub located on the outskirts of a village on the coast of Mayo. It's an autumn evening around 1900. There's a bar, a few pieces of banged-up furniture, and shelves sagging under the weight of bottles and jugs.

As the play opens, Pegeen Mike is planning her wedding to Shawn Keogh, a timid milksop who is her cousin. Apparently, marriageable men are in short supply on this wild stretch of the coast.

In comes a boisterous trio led by Pegeen's father, who owns the pub, and two of his drinking companions. There's talk of a stranger heading this way; he may be a dangerous criminal. Shawn is so afraid that he runs out the door and out of his coat, leaving Pegeen's dad holding it for him, drawing laughter from the audience.

It's a great sight gag, and it prepares the way for Christy Mahon's entrance. Bobby Colman certainly looked the part as he stumbled onto the stage, his hair mussed, clothes soiled and wrinkled from sleeping rough, cheeks unshaven and streaked with dirt.

Bobby—that is, Christy—announces he's on the run from the police, and everyone in the pub gathers round, eager to hear his story. What crime did you commit, asks Pegeen's dad—was it larceny?

No, says Christy, something bigger than that.

Did you chase after young girls?

I'm a decent lad, he protests.

Attack your landlord?

No, he says, those are everyday crimes.

Did you marry three wives?

Not even one, he answers.

At that, Pegeen perks up. Teasing him, she claims he's done nothing at all and raises a broom to chase him away. Christy bursts out that he killed his poor father for threatening him like that a week ago Tuesday.

Instead of recoiling, Christy's listeners gather around him. It's not every day that a man kills his father. They want to hear all the gory details. Rising to the occasion, Christy relates how he was tired of his father bossing him around and how he hit him over the head with a spade while they were digging potatoes. He embellishes the tale as if he were spinning an epic yarn, and Pegeen is taken by him.

In the next scene, Christy woos her and is in turn pursued by the Widow Quinn. The two women have a tug of war over Christy, much to his delight. At the end of the act, he wonders out loud why he never thought of killing his father before.

There was an uneasy stirring as the audience tried to absorb these unexpected plot developments. While the laughter continued, it had a nervous edge.

As the lights came up and the curtains closed for a brief interval between the acts, there was a buzz of conversation in the hall.

"How do you like it so far?" Toby asked Mom and Dad.

"When does Angie come on?" asked Dad.

"I think in the next act," said Toby.

"The acting is excellent," said Mom.

I agreed. Bobby was doing a great job in a demanding role.

"I still don't understand what makes him so appealing," said Dad, meaning Christy.

"Let's see what happens," said Mom, patting him on the knee.

While my parents were chatting, my thoughts were elsewhere. I was thinking of the Irishman who attacked his English landlady and was hidden by the Achill islanders when the police came looking for him. With Michael O'Hara on the loose, were islanders sheltering him as well? If O'Hara *was* the killer of Frank Hickey, was I in any danger from him? The events of a century ago suddenly felt contemporary, and this strange play, with its mixture of comedy and violence, was disturbing me to the bone.

The houselights blinked and dimmed, signaling that we were ready for Act Two.

It's the next morning. Christy has spent the night in the pub and is sprucing up, admiring himself in a looking glass. Three gushing village girls come in bearing gifts to win his favor. One of them is Angie. There's no mistaking her; her height gives her away. One girl presents Christy with eggs, the other offers him butter. Then Angie gets her moment. She's brought a pullet that was run over by the curate's car last night—in other words, roadkill. She pulls a rubber chicken out of her basket and says, "Feel the fat of that breast, mister." It's Angie's only line, but she makes the most of it, getting a laugh. I mark her debut on the Irish stage as a success.

As the act continues, the Widow Quinn returns. She and the three groupies prevail upon Christy to tell his story again. Each time he does, the tale becomes more exaggerated. This time he says he split the old man's skull down to his gullet.

As if on cue, there's a rap on the door. Christy peeks out and staggers back. The audience gasps, for it's the old man himself, head bandaged, but very much alive. Christy hides behind the door while his father berates him as a coward who got in a lucky blow and ran away.

It was time for the intermission. The houselights came up, and the hall echoed to animated conversation as perplexed members of the audience headed for the bar.

"Well, I didn't expect that," muttered Dad.

Mom brushed aside his remark. "What did you think of our Angie?" she preened. "Wasn't she great?"

"She's a natural on stage," said Toby.

"Did you hear the laugh she got with that rubber chicken?" Mom went on.

"She did fine," Dad agreed. "Is she in the next act too?"

"There's a crowd scene," said Toby. "She'd be in that. I don't recall if she has any more speaking lines." He stood up. "I'm going to get something to drink. Does anybody else want something?"

"If they have a Coke, I'd like one," said Mom.

"Me too," I said.

Dad said, "Let's go over and say hello to Laura and Emily. See how they're doing."

"I think I'll wait here for Toby to get back," said Mom. "I don't feel like standing."

Dad and I jostled our way to the aisle and walked up a few rows to where Laura and Emily were sitting. "Oh, hello," said Laura. "That was a surprise to see Angie up there. How did she get a part in the play?"

"She's been dating the guy who plays Christy," I admitted.

She looked surprised but not disapproving. "He's very good. And cute too. Don't you think so, Emily?"

Emily nodded and offered a weak smile. She didn't look well. Her skin was pasty and she seemed nervous.

"Are you all right, Emily?" I asked.

"I've been feeling a little queasy. It'll pass."

"Can we get you anything?"

She shook her head. "I'll be all right, thanks."

"I don't think it's anything serious," said Laura. "She gets these moments when she's nauseous and dizzy, but they don't last long."

Seeing Toby approaching with two paper cups, I said, "When my stomach gets queasy, sometimes a Coke helps settle it. Would you like one?" I took my drink from Toby and passed it to her. She sipped and said thanks.

We stood there for an awkward moment. Laura ventured, "It's an odd play, isn't it? I don't know what to make of it."

"I don't either," said Dad.

"I don't care for it very much," said Emily.

"Maybe that's because you're not feeling well," I said.

"Maybe." She looked down at the cup.

The houselights blinked. "Time to get back to our seats," said Toby.

"We'll see you after the play. I hope you feel better," I said to Emily. But something was wrong, something that couldn't be fixed by a Coke.

"What did they think of Angie?" asked Mom, as we retook our seats.

"They thought she was very good," said Dad. "Emily's not feeling well, though."

"Oh?" said Mom, looking toward her. We couldn't say more, as the play was about to resume.

Act Three opens with Christy being hailed as "the champion playboy of the western world." He's won the mule races on the beach below. Pegeen, smitten by his fine words and athletic deeds, agrees to marry him—just as his battered father catches up with him. He knocks Christy down and tells the crowd that Christy's story is a lie. Yet there's another twist: Christy gambles on winning the crowd back by turning what was a lie into the truth. He picks up a spade and chases the old man out the door. There's a great noise and a yell offstage—and then silence. Christy returns alone. What's happened? Has he killed his father for real this time?

I didn't find out that night. Emily rose from her seat, crying "No! No!" She pushed her way to the aisle as if trying to escape the theater. She lurched over the feet of the man on the end of the row and fell, bringing the performance to a halt.

After a moment of confusion, the actors withdrew and the lights came up. The director, a middle-aged woman, stepped to the front of the stage. She asked if there was a doctor in the house (there wasn't) and announced that the play would resume after a five-minute intermission. Meanwhile, Emily had recovered sufficiently to get to her feet and shake off assistance. She stubbornly insisted she was all right. Aunt Laura and I had reached her side. "Take me home," she said to her mother.

I offered to come with them and took Emily by the elbow to steady her as we moved toward the exit. Passing our row, I grabbed my rain jacket and asked Toby to stay with Mom and Dad and finish the play.

It wasn't Christy I was thinking of as we left the theater. It was Claudius in *Hamlet* when he sees his crime acted out before his eyes and halts the play within the play. Was Emily's reaction similar? Did she see herself as Christy when he raised his spade against his father? Or was she simply overwhelmed by the events of the past week? I had to find out.

19

RAIN WAS SO HEAVY that we stopped at the door, instinctively recoiling, but Emily was in no shape to stay. With one arm, I tented my jacket over her head; with the other I steered her outside and down the stairs. "This way," said Laura, heading out ahead of us at a run, fishing in her purse for car keys.

The slanting rain splattered against the hood I had made for Emily, as we staggered, bound to each other, toward Laura's car. She had the lights on and the motor running, ready to move as soon as I could get Emily and myself into the back seat. In the second before the door closed and the interior lights went out, I saw Emily's tight grimace. My body clenched in reaction, but my brain began its assessment. Was that rage on her face, or guilt, or devastation? I kept thinking of the line from *Hamlet*: "The play's the thing wherein I'll catch the conscience of the King."

Blessedly, compassion and family feeling kicked in. I rearranged my jacket as a blanket over Emily's chest and tucked the edges behind her. I sat by her, thigh to thigh, and warmed her hands with mine, murmuring the universal bromide: "It'll be all right, it'll be all right."

I saw my aunt looking in the mirror to check on her daughter. That very morning, she had wished I could comfort Emily, and her wish was coming true, but under unwanted circumstances. She hadn't envisioned Emily falling apart in public.

"See if you can get her to sleep," Laura said. Emily was rigid, as if stuck on one emotion or one thought. Her mother was right: sleep would be a relief. But it didn't come.

When the car stopped in front of her house, Emily came to life, throwing aside my jacket and pushing me away. She stumbled out of the car, righted herself, walked quickly to the front door, and grasped the handle. When it didn't give, she called, "Mama! Open the door!" Laura hurried, key in hand, while I gathered everyone's belongings and closed the car doors. By then, they were in the house and Emily was shouting something like "Get out of here!"

I hurried to the house, to come to Laura's aid, but on the threshold I realized that I had misheard. Emily was saying, "Get *her* out of here!" Meaning me.

I halted. Laura, with her back to me, replied urgently, "We can handle this, Emily. Calm down."

Emily saw me and pulled away from her mother. Aunt Laura turned. If she thought I had overheard, she didn't let on. She walked toward me and thanked me for my help. I made the usual reply while handing over her purse, still open from the scramble to get out the house key.

"You look better," I said to Emily. "Are you all right?"

"I'll be—don't." In her agitation, she dropped the finger-sized old-fashioned house key. It clanged on the floor, startling us all.

I picked it up and gestured for Emily to sit on the couch. "Maybe you spoke too soon," I said, in the calmest tone I could muster. "Let's sit and catch our breaths." I took a chair opposite the couch, and Emily complied.

Her mother remained standing and said, "We've ruined your evening already, Nora. Let me drive you home and we'll give Emily some space. How about that?"

Emily nodded, but I stayed seated and said to her, "I think it would be better if we stayed with you a while. You're not yourself yet. And besides, Toby's coming for me when the play's over. He'll take my parents home and come straight here."

Mother and daughter looked at each other, without speaking. I let them be. After a time, I said to Laura, "Maybe it would be a good idea to make Emily some tea."

Emily shook her head and said, "No, no. Stay here, Mama. I don't want anything." Laura went to sit by her.

"What upset you?" I asked. "Was it something in the play?"

Laura replied, "Of course it was something in the play. All that talk of beating a man over the head. Neither of us needed to hear that."

Over her mother's protest, Emily said, "They treated it as if it were funny. It's not funny. Not one bit."

"No, it's not," I replied, pushing ahead, "not after what happened to your dad. The play must have made you relive that night, but maybe what you need is to talk about it."

Laura shot back, "You know more about it than we do. You actually saw the place where it happened. We weren't allowed to see even that."

"Yes, I saw the crime scene, but I don't know what drove Uncle Bert into the night to a place it's hard to walk in, even in the day. What you told the guards doesn't make sense to me. He may have liked to walk in the Deserted Village, but not in the dark. It's not a place for an evening stroll. Something must have happened to send him out there."

"It was an argument," said Emily.

Her mother flinched. "Bert and I . . . had a few words," she said, her voice faltering.

"About what?" I asked. Laura paused and looked questioningly at her daughter. With a nod, Emily signaled her permission.

"The business. It's ruined," said Laura. "I'd just found out."

"Bert told you that, the night he died?"

"No, he was too much of a coward to tell me. The business is a shambles, and he didn't tell me."

"Are you sure it's that bad?" I asked. "Uncle Bert didn't get where he was without organizational skills. He wouldn't let his affairs become a mess."

Laura was too dignified to say I didn't know what I was talking about, but her face made the statement for her. She paused, and I sensed she was calculating whether it was worth the effort, or safe, to explain things.

"When I met Bert, it looked like his business was expanding. He owned rental properties, and he made a profit from them, but he wasn't content with a steady income. He craved the excitement of building. At first it was housing in the city, then shopping malls in the suburbs, then towers of offices in the financial district. He was always moving ahead of his actual wealth, mortgaging one property to build another. I don't know when he realized he'd hit a wall. Maybe he never let himself know. But he reached the end of his credit with the banks a long time ago. He's been funding his building projects with a Ponzi scheme, and it's crashing as we speak."

"I had no idea," I said. "You always looked so prosperous. Did you keep some personal money separate, so you could cover your expenses even if the business went down?"

"Ha!" she blurted. "I wish."

"Then how did you keep it all going?"

"*He* kept it all going by pulling the wool over my eyes. I believed in him. We met when I was getting a grip on my husband's estate. Doug had invested in one of Bert's projects. Bert advised me to leave the money there, and then he convinced me to bankroll another project, and before I knew it we were married and I let him manage our money. I suppose I realized he had a credit line to every account Doug and I once shared, but I really didn't give it a thought. I raised Emily, tended Bert, entertained his clients, and served on boards. There was always enough money in the accounts I drew on. Meanwhile, Bert was steadily depleting the funds that Doug left me. Bert built his reputation for financial genius on Doug's money."

"It must have been a significant amount, if it bankrolled Barnes Properties."

"It was. And it should have ensured stability. But here we are, and the company's crumbling."

"I'm so sorry," I said, reaching out to squeeze her hand. This time, she let me offer sympathy. My hand rested on hers as I asked, "What does this mean for Emily?"

Laura pulled back her hand, drew it to her chest, and clasped the other hand, in a gesture of pent-up anger. Her pale cheeks took color. Then she spoke directly to Emily, who woke as from a stupor to listen.

"I'll never forgive Bert for what he's done to you. I thought it was so generous of him to bring you into the business, but now I see he's brought you down with him. It's worse than that. He doesn't have to face anything. You're left to manage the collapse of his empire."

Emily sat up straighter, bracing herself with her hands on the cushion. She said, "I don't know if I can, Mama. I don't know *scat* about the money! Daddy wouldn't let me near the financials. He said my job was to woo new clients and keep the old ones coming back. I was never put on the management team, and I never saw the books. Daddy said it was better that way, because the top guys wouldn't worry that the little heiress was going to take charge."

"Then I will," said Laura. "I won't be the first widow to save a business, and you'll be right with me. We'll take it project by project, starting with the ones on Achill. It won't be easy without Frank, but we'll do it."

"I'm sorry to ask you, Laura, but did Frank know all this?"

"Frank's the one who discovered the truth about this latest scheme and told me. He found out too late, after he and his friends had invested in the death train project." She shook her head. "You're supposed to do 'due diligence' *before* you invest, not after. Frank didn't investigate Barnes Properties until he got tipped off by one of his friends on the county council. They look into a builder's liquidity before they give permission to build, and they were concerned by what they learned."

I could just see it—Frank getting a phone call with the bad news and confronting Bert. Bert blowing him off. Frank waiting till dark to act on his anger. If it happened that way, Frank was a slick pretender. During his condolence call to Aunt Laura, as well as at the pub, he made Bert out to be a business genius. That was just a week ago.

I asked, "Do you think Frank could have killed Bert over this?"

Laura looked to the side, as if thinking. I wished I could remember that "tell" they talk about: if you look one direction, you're recalling; if you look the other, you're cooking up a lie.

She said, "Possibly. He was certainly angry. His friends had invested in the project on Frank's recommendation. And he may have been concerned for me."

In case Emily didn't know about her mother's affair, I didn't mention it. "I still don't understand why Bert was in the Deserted Village that night. You said it was because of your argument. What happened?"

"I told him he was an arrogant fool. While his debts were coming due back home, he kept his ego inflated with these silly projects. He was playing around with toy trains while my fortune and Emily's were being wiped out!" She added, as an afterthought: "Frank's too."

Emily jumped in. "Daddy didn't care about Frank. What made him crack was when you accused him of betraying me. He did, too. He lied to me about everything, and he made me his tool. My job was to convince clients how successful we were, but we were really going under, and I didn't know." Her anger was finally showing.

I asked, "What do you mean, it made him crack?"

"He'd been drinking during the argument and by then he'd lost control. He shoved her," she said, her voice rising. "He slammed Mama against the wall, and then he ran out the door. He didn't even check to see if she was okay."

"So you ran out after him and you caught him in the ruin and you picked up a stone and hit him."

She stood up. "No, it wasn't like that! I just wanted to confront him."

"Stop!" Laura hissed.

I didn't know whether she was addressing me or Emily. But I pushed on. "Emily. Did you hit your father with a stone?"

Laura shot her arm across Emily's face, as if to fend off an attacker. "Leave her alone!" she said. "She's talking nonsense."

"No," I said. "She needs to get out what's bothering her."

"I wanted to tell him what a bastard he was," said Emily.

Uncle Bert the bastard. Even Emily thought of him like that.

Laura barked "Be quiet!" but Emily spoke as if she hadn't heard. "I can't undo it. I didn't mean to do it, but I can't undo it."

Her anguish drew my pity. Impulsively, I said, "We can help you get through this, Emily."

Laura scoffed. "Help her? You call this helping her?"

"Shutting her up is not going to help her. You can't hide something like this from the guards. They've got DNA and fiber analysis and who knows what. She'll be caught. We can't stop that from happening. But we can help her build a defense that will keep her out of prison. There must be a story here. She didn't intend to kill Bert. That's what she says, and don't you believe her?"

Emily whispered, "Tell her, Mom." She held her head in her hands.

Laura, openmouthed with exasperation, looked at her daughter, then at me. Eyes flashing, she said, "If you want to know what really happened, ask your mother!"

"What?" My mouth fell open.

"You heard me. Ask your mother. This is as much about her as it is about Emily."

"I don't understand." And I didn't, but the blow hit me again—Mom, as Bert's killer. I managed: "Are you saying that my mother was there when Bert was killed? Why would she be?"

Emily picked up her head. "I don't know, but I heard screams and I ran toward them. I found my father struggling with your mother in one of the ruins." Her hands were waving in front of her, acting out what she had seen.

"All right," I said automatically. It was certainly not all right. "The three of you were at the Deserted Village. You saw my mother arguing with Uncle Bert. Then what?"

"I shouted at them, but they didn't stop. Then I saw that Daddy had his hands around your mother's throat. He was choking her. I tried to pull him away but he flung me aside."

"And then?"

"I took a rock from the rubble."

"And you struck him on the head."

"I didn't mean to kill him."

"Emily saved your mother's life, is what happened," Aunt Laura said. "Since then it's been a nightmare, one horror after another."

"Why didn't you go to the guards and tell them it was a matter of saving a life?"

"Because it would be too easy for them to assume that Emily hit Bert in anger, after the argument we had," said Laura. "He ruined her, so she killed him. That would be the story they'd seize on: murder and revenge. So we agreed to say nothing."

"My mom agreed too?"

"Yes."

"And when Frank Hickey was killed, you hoped the guards would pin Bert's murder on him?"

Laura's silence was the answer.

"Who killed Frank, Laura?"

"I swear I don't know." She looked completely in earnest. "But I'm asking you to keep our secret."

"It's too late for that," I said.

Emily stood up and swayed. "It's over, Mama. I've ruined my life, and I'll end up in prison. I'd be better off dead!"

"Don't say such a thing," Laura cried. But before she could block her, Emily bolted for the door.

"Go after her," Laura implored. "She's desperate, she could do anything."

I whipped my jacket from the back of a chair and chased my cousin into the night.

The rain was now a drizzle, but gray fog had rolled in from the ocean, making it hard to see more than a yard ahead. I called Emily's name and thought I heard movement heading down the lane, so I followed the sound. My head was spinning, trying to make sense of what I had just learned—that Mom was at the Deserted Village struggling with Uncle Bert on the night of the murder. I couldn't imagine why Mom would be there, but I certainly could see her in a fight with Bert. Did Emily really save her from being killed by Bert? If so, Mom had kept Emily's secret—their secret—from our family and the police. I called out again but my voice was muffled by rain and fog. I jogged on until I reached the road. I decided to turn toward Slievemore Mountain, and sure enough, I heard a runner ahead of me. I guessed that Emily was returning to the Deserted Village, driven to revisit the scene of horror.

The country road had no lights, and I feared running into the deep ditch that edged the road. When I reached the parking lot of the village, I was temporarily disoriented, but turning around, I saw the lights of Laura's house, and then I knew the tented crime scene was somewhere above me on the slope, though it could be in any one of several directions. A light source might help. I didn't have a flashlight, but I did have a phone in my jacket. When I pressed the right icon, it created a triangle of light. Holding the phone like a lantern with my arm extended, I made my way slowly up the hill, from one ruin to another. Almost every cottage had lost its roof and provided no shelter from the weather. Several, though, retained odd bits of overhang and offered refuge, however slight, in the corners of the structure. I was drawn to these. I would step through a break in the rubble that had once been a doorway, shine my light into the corners looking for a huddled figure, and move on.

Halfway up the slope, I came to one of the larger ruins and saw that someone had been camping in it. My phone light picked up a bedroll with a backpack and tin can sitting next to it. My first impression was that the bedroll was empty. I was wrong. It sprang to life and a snarling figure hurled himself at me, knocking me on my back and sending my phone sliding away. Michael O'Hara straddled my chest and pinned my wrists to the ground. I struggled, and his head mirrored my movements. He was trying to make out who I was, and when he did, he pressed me even more tightly to the ground. "You're the bitch who put the gardai on to me. How did you find me here?"

I squirmed but couldn't budge. "I wasn't looking for you," I managed to get out. "I'm looking for someone else."

"Who's with you?"

"Nobody."

He glanced around to confirm that I was alone, but he couldn't have seen much. Beyond the eroded walls of the ruined cottage, all was dark.

Inside, the phone, fallen screen side up, illuminated O'Hara's grinning face. I smelled whiskey on his breath. "You shouldn't have butted in," he growled.

"Let me go. You'll make things worse for yourself when they catch you."

"*If* they catch me. I don't think they will." He reached around to the back of his waistband and withdrew a knife. He had to release one of my wrists to do so, and that gave me a chance. I shoved my hand under his chin as hard as I could. Lying on my back, I didn't have much leverage, but it was enough to throw him off balance and give me room to bring my knee to my chest. I kicked with all my strength. The blow landed squarely on his shoulder and knocked him back. I rolled out from under O'Hara, got to my feet, and dashed out, hoping that the rain, fog, and darkness would provide cover.

Now it was a game of cat and mouse, and I was the one with the short whiskers. I ran into the closest ruin and hid myself in a corner until I heard him run by. Then I lit out in the opposite direction, sloshing through the wet grass. But I heard him stop and turn. He knew where I was, and he was coming after me. To throw him off my track, I zigzagged downhill between the empty cottages. He was relentless, though. Panting, I pushed myself against the side of a ruin and waited for him to go by. The cold, moist stone pressed against my hands, and needles of rain stung my face. I heard him before I saw him. He ran by but slipped when he sensed my presence, giving me just enough of an advantage to start out again. This time I headed uphill. I weaved between the ruins, but my strength was giving out. When I thought I had built a lead, I chose the ruin ahead of me and bundled myself inside. I made no sound, and as the minutes went by, I thought I might be safe, until the light from my cell phone, wielded by O'Hara, caught me in its beam like an escapee in a prison yard. "There you are," he said in a voice as cold as the night. And I saw the knife in his hand.

If he thought I was trapped, he was wrong. Without walls, the ruin offered a way out in several directions. I stood up, turned, and scrambled over the rubble. Then I ran like hell down the hill. O'Hara followed, cursing behind me. I was increasing the distance between us when my ankle twisted on the slippery ground and I went down in agony. I braced for the attack.

O'Hara loomed over me. But Toby was behind him. He launched himself at O'Hara and they tumbled in the grass, locked in struggle. Toby grappled for the knife, slamming O'Hara's wrist against a boulder. The knife dropped. Both men got to their feet, but Toby kicked the knife away. Yet O'Hara landed a roundhouse punch and Toby went down. O'Hara took a step toward me but paused with indecision. Fight or flee? With Toby on the scene, he decided to run. He scampered down the slope, disappearing long before the sounds of his flight faded.

I limped over to Toby, who was sitting up, rubbing his chin. "Got me with a sucker punch," he mumbled.

"Never mind that," I said. "How did you find me?"

"Laura sent me after you, and when I got here I saw the light from your phone. Good thing I did."

"What should we do about O'Hara?"

"Call the guards, and tell them he's at the Deserted Village and on the run. They ought to be able to pick him up. Tell them one of his friends might be here too. I thought I heard something in one of the cottages up there as I ran by."

I made the call to the guards, who promised to send a search team for O'Hara, and we went to investigate what Toby had heard. He had to support me to keep the weight off my sprained ankle. As we climbed (or rather he climbed, I hobbled), I told him Emily could be on the hill. We paused every few feet to listen. Then I heard it too: the sound of whimpering. We looked into one ruin, then another, until we found her. Emily was sitting on the dirt floor of the cottage softly sobbing, her legs drawn up to her chest and her head bowed on her knees. I sat down and put my arms around her. "It's over, Emily," I said. "We'll take you home."

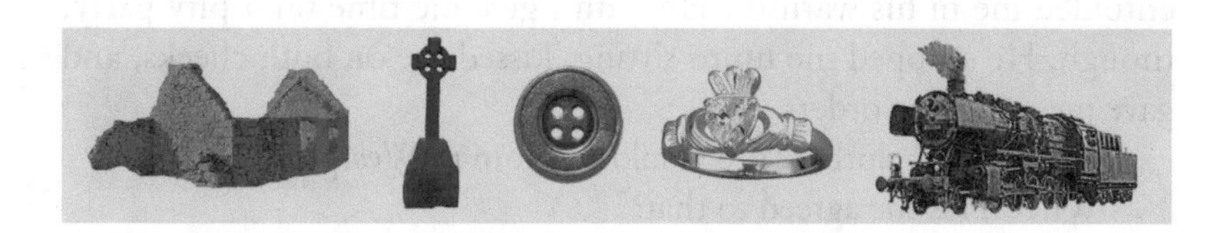

20

IN THE MORNING, Laura drove Emily to Westport to sign a confession; it was what she wanted to do. It would be up to the Director of Public Prosecution to decide whether to charge her with murder or with a lesser crime such as involuntary manslaughter, but almost certainly she would stand trial. At least that's what Toby thought. He had spent the night hunched over his laptop, searching for laws, precedents, and procedures that would apply in County Mayo. We weren't expecting to find a close parallel in this thinly populated "west county," but we were stunned by the number of bashings and knifings between fathers and children, especially when we widened the search to all Ireland. Christy Mahon had his twenty-first-century counterparts, and they weren't all sons either.

Emily's defense was one issue; Mom's was another. While I napped between three and five in the morning, Toby kept going, looking for angles on how Mom's conduct would be viewed. He woke me at dawn saying that, just as in the States, Mom could be charged with withholding information, since she had witnessed the crime but hadn't said so when questioned.

"Oh, God," I said, burying my face in my pillow. Toby lowered himself onto the small space between me and the edge of the bed and enfolded me in his warmth. He didn't give me time for a pity party, though. He scooped me up to sitting, kissed me on both cheeks, and gave me marching orders.

"Get on your clothes. We're taking Mom to Westport."

"What? Has she agreed to that?"

He grunted and said, "Get going."

Though I groggily got out of bed, I said, "That wasn't a yes. Don't think I didn't notice."

While I found clothes and washed up, Toby gave me his report. He paced in the cramped space between the bed and the bathroom door, which I kept half-open, so as not to lose a word. He said that before daylight he started tiptoeing into our bedroom, pulling back the curtains to see if there was light next door. At six sharp, the kitchen brightened, and he called Dad's cell. Together they made a plan. We would give Mom some time to consider what she would tell the guards, and then we would go to the station, all four of us. I wasn't so sure Mom would welcome my presence, but Dad was grateful for Toby's offer to drive. Dad was pretty fractured, Toby said. "It's not enough that his brother was killed. His own wife was there and, in a sense, her being there led to what happened."

"Did Dad really say that?" I asked. I couldn't believe it. Dad's devoted to Mom.

Toby closed his eyes, as if reliving the call. Then his lids popped open and he said, "Not in so many words. It was implied."

"Or inferred." I was pissed. "*You* may think she caused the murder, but Dad doesn't, I'll tell you that."

Toby has the patience of a Freudian shrink. He kept silent. I couldn't see him, but I knew he had that "Take your time—we have forty minutes" look. I applied a brush to my hair and considered. Then I asked, "What's going to happen to Emily? Laura's afraid that the police will think Emily attacked Bert because he ruined her life."

"They might have a case," Toby admitted. "Emily picked up a rock to keep him from choking your Mom. That's what a good lawyer would point out. But would she have hit him as hard as she did—hard enough to kill him—if they hadn't had an argument that night? Who knows? Motivation is difficult to calibrate."

"I don't believe she meant to kill him," I said. "Emily was angry, but not killing-angry. She's not the type." Was Mom? It wasn't beyond believing, or at least not by me. But she didn't do it, and I needn't have been thinking so all this time. I didn't say that to Toby. I guess I was ashamed of my lack of faith in Mom. Over the years, I've let Toby get to know me, and he undoubtedly felt my shame, but I couldn't voice my guilty thoughts just then.

I emerged from the bathroom and said, "Let's go."

When we arrived, Dad was washing dishes and Mom was at the table, writing on a yellow pad. Toby sat next to Mom and spoke with her quietly. I took a dish towel and joined Dad at the sink. The flow of tap water and the clanking of dishes muffled Toby's words with Mom. I didn't say much to Dad. His fear for Mom was shaking him so much that his hand trembled as he handed me a dribbling cup. He asked, "What'll they do to her?" His voice was faint.

I couldn't fake optimism, not with my earnest, suffering father.

"I don't know, Dad. They might arrest Emily, but I hope they'll see Mom wasn't responsible for Uncle Bert's death."

"Wasn't responsible?" he said, his voice rising. Startled by his own voice, he turned back to the sink. Looking down at the soapy sponge in his hand, he whispered, "She was fighting him. We can't let them know that."

Mom spoke up in the rousing tone she used to use when telling us kids to get a move on. "Jim, come. Let's get this over with."

She got in the rear of our car, with Dad. I felt uncomfortable sitting up front, next to Toby. It felt backward, as if we were the parents, and Mom and Dad were the children. A wave of tenderness for them washed through me. They were struggling, enmeshed in death and divided in loyalties. Dad was mourning his brother; yet he was anxious for his wife, who unwittingly occasioned the death. Mom was determined to protect Emily from going to prison for killing Bert; yet she must have felt compassion for Dad, who was grieving over Bert's death.

Mom was a cipher to me, as was often the case. Her love for Dad was always clear in her expression when she smiled at him; in her body, when she swayed toward his; and in her words, which always held respect. Otherwise, apart from her rare "witch tirades"—and, I admit, her verbal tangle with Bert at the Galway party qualified as one—Mom generally gave little sign of strong emotion. She was direct and decisive. In most matters she led the family, and Dad followed in full contentment. But she wasn't much for hugging, heart-talk, or what she called "brooding." In fact, I often saw her cut Dad short when he expressed disappointment or sadness. I certainly felt barred from emoting in front of her. Anyhow, at that moment, I had little idea how she was feeling.

In one way, Toby's like Mom. He shows more empathy than she does, but like her he's focused on what needs to be done. So when we got to the station, it didn't surprise me that he strode purposefully to the reception counter, right along with Mom, while Dad and I looked on. The female officer on duty called Sergeant Flynn, who came out to the lobby to talk to us. I had a good feeling about Sergeant Flynn, maybe because he had been gentle when he and the inspector questioned Mom at the house. He was kind again now, reassuring us with the news of O'Hara's arrest. My attacker had been found in the bogs between the Deserted Village and the shore, where Toby and I had hiked the other morning. He was in the cells right now, held for the murder of Frank Hickey. I shivered, surprising myself. I was afraid of his nearness a room or two away. I was more unsettled by his attack on me than I had realized.

Flynn kept going, saying O'Hara had confessed to Frank's murder when they took his ring to be checked for Frank's DNA. He knew he was well caught, and now he was claiming a crime of passion. His story was that he was driving by the Kildownet graveyard with a bag of groceries in his car when he saw Hickey poking around the graves of the victims of the 1894 drowning. He took offense, got out of his car, and they fought. He knocked Frank out with a punch to the face and dragged him into the church so that passersby wouldn't see. Then he got the idea of forcing a loaf of brown bread, which he had in the car, into Hickey's mouth. He meant to draw a comparison between Hickey and that landlord during the Famine who was dispatched by a loaf of bread, but not to kill him, or so O'Hara claimed. He said he stuck a wad of bread into Frank's mouth, thinking that when Frank came to he would cough it up and get the message. But Frank choked on the loaf and died of asphyxiation. Flynn said that to have caused asphyxiation, O'Hara would have had to shove the bread deep into Frank's throat. Now O'Hara was under lock and key. He could tell his tale to the judge.

Mom interrupted. "Did my niece Emily come by this morning?"

Flynn blinked. Maybe he realized he had been prattling on about a solved murder when an unsolved murder was still under investigation. "Em. I believe she's in back with her mother, waiting for the inspector." Flynn looked at the clock. "He'll be here soon. He's not an early riser." He blushed, perhaps realizing how little his boss would have approved this remark or anything else he had divulged to us. He backed up (literally and figuratively) and said, "Will that be all, then?"

Mom stepped forward. "No, it isn't. Please tell the inspector I have a statement to make, related to the Barnes case." She stood tall, with the impassive dignity of a soldier on parade.

"You do? Right. Just a moment." He swiveled and sought the door to the back offices, giving a quick eye to the guard at the reception desk. It seemed the young woman had been listening to this interchange with great interest. She leaned forward across the counter, the better to keep watch over us while the sergeant was gone.

Dad huddled with Mom. The lobby was such a small space that every word was audible, but he whispered anyhow. "I'll be with you. Don't be afraid." He tried to bring Mom into a hug, but she resisted.

She said firmly, "I'm not afraid, Jim. And I don't want you with me." When she saw Dad's reaction, she reworded her demand. "It's my story, and I want to tell it." Now Dad really looked hurt. "Just let me do this by myself," Mom said. "I'll be distracted if you're there."

When Flynn returned, that's how it went. Mom disappeared and we were left in the cramped hall, with two folding chairs and a bulletin board.

"You two, sit," said Toby. "She's right, you know. She needs to concentrate."

I added feebly, "They probably wouldn't have let you be with her, Dad. They didn't question Toby and me in the same room, even though we were talking about finding Frank's body, together."

He thought for a moment. "They should be talking to me too, then. It was my brother who died. And I can testify that Mom was with me at the time."

I held my tongue, almost literally. My hand went to my mouth, to keep back what I shouldn't say.

We stayed in Westport for an early lunch at the pub by the river, facing the train bridge that used to carry workers from Westport to Achill. Now it carried neither trains nor autos. From our table by the window, I could see a club of bicyclists in matching outfits whizzing across the bridge. If Bert had had his way, the Achill line would have been reactivated and the bicyclists would be on the streets, mourning the Great Western Greenway.

"Mourning." That word brought me back to the present and my family's grief. We were eating salmon patties, the daily special, and there wasn't much talk among us. I was grateful for the noisy family at the next table. The father was "helping" his daughter finish her ice cream, and she was screeching in protest. Her older brothers were squabbling over possession of a mobile phone. The mother was feeding the baby spoonfuls of melted ice cream. That was a normal family on a normal day.

Mom sampled her fish cakes calmly, while Dad devoured his rapidly, as if there would be a reward when he finished. Toby and I picked at our food. We were all waiting for Mom to talk about her interview, but she wasn't giving. She apparently thought she had said all that was needed, back at the station. That was: "Done. I signed a statement."

As we rolled over the gravel in front of our cottages, Dad declared he was taking a siesta. We are both champion nappers. We share a hibernating instinct, pronounced in times of stress. Mom and Angie are the opposite; they're most active when most troubled. Though I felt myself drooping, I was determined to get outside with Mom while Dad napped. Our distance from each other in the midst of this turmoil was becoming intolerable. I wanted to know what was happening inside her, and I hoped she might talk on a walk. So I waited till Dad went off to the bedroom, and I proposed that we take the walk I had done with Dad, down to the beach at Dugort.

She hesitated. I said, "Mom, please. I want to be friends again. I don't want Uncle Bert's death to tear us apart." She looked away, her sober face set in marble. Nonetheless, I spoke again. "We can't understand each other if we don't communicate. Please. Come for a walk with me. We'll see if we can talk."

She looked toward the bedroom and said, "Give me a minute." I was left to sit in the kitchen, while she . . . debated whether to come? talked to Dad? pulled herself together? I don't know. But we did walk.

Days ago, Dad had walked with me in contemplative silence till he finally spoke when we reached the beach. This day, Mom strode aggressively, the better, it seemed to me, to forestall conversation. I had to jog to keep up with her. Halfway down the mile-long decline to the shore, she stopped in front of the gate to a gray church hidden in the shade of a stand of trees, rare on the island. I caught up with her and read the faded plaque attached to the gate, thinking that maybe we would begin by discussing what the plaque said about Achill's relationship to the Church of Ireland. That could get us started on a neutral topic, a hot topic in Irish history but not as fraught as the Barnes family troubles. But Mom countered my ploy with one of her own.

"You should try interval training. At your age, you shouldn't be out of breath." This wasn't exactly girl talk, but Mom's tone wasn't critical, more informational. Maybe concerned, but I wasn't sure about that. "You could run on that long beach you have. Angie told me about it. If you invited me, I'd come and show you my morning routine."

"I'd *love* it if you'd come!" I nearly shouted. Then, puzzled, I added, "Do you actually do interval training?"

With a small smile and a nod, she resumed her swift pace toward Dugort. We didn't speak till we reached the water, close to the spot where Dad had told me about his childhood with Bert.

"Let's walk the beach," Mom said. I felt as if the queen had invited me to tea.

Wind-dried sand slowed us down, and that improved the chance of talking. Mom started. "You always went where you didn't belong. I'd find you in the attic, reading Grandma's love letters to Grandpa or dressing up in my peasant skirts from the sixties." We both smiled at the memories. "Remember when you climbed into the old furnace in the basement—nearly scared me to death." I stayed quiet, while we skirted the smelly carcass of a beached seal pup.

"You won't rest till you know, so I'd better just tell you. But you'll have to promise you won't speak of this to anyone but Dad. Can you promise?"

I have a rule against promising not to tell. That kind of promise ruins friendships and rots families. However, this was my mother, under duress. "Can there be an exception?" I asked. "Toby?"

"I trust Toby. Just tell him to keep mum." She changed course, turning toward a log at the back of the beach. She sat down on the log and tilted her head to ask me to join her. When I was settled, she began. "The night Bert died, I was in a state. The things he said the day before at the party were intolerable. Awful things about Dad's father. Granddad was a hardworking, capable man. He was *not* confused in his old age. And he damn well wasn't a drunk. Bert only said that to justify taking over Granddad's business, and the mortgage to his house, and finally all his money. It's a terrible thing to have done, and an ugly thing to justify with slanders. Poor Grammy. If she knew what Bert said, she would be so hurt."

"What did you do, Mom? The night he died?"

"Always to the point, aren't you?" There wasn't any sting in this. She was laughing, almost. "I drove to Bert's house, and I was going to chew him out in front of Laura. At the Jubilee I was too furious to make my case clearly. I had time to think it through overnight, and I wanted to put it to both of them, the whole story, the way Dad told it to me."

"Why didn't Dad confront Bert himself?" I knew the answer, of course, and Mom knew I did. She ignored the question.

"I was at their door, working up the steam to knock, when I heard them yelling—Laura and Bert and Emily. I went closer to the window, to listen. There was a crash and a thump and then Bert came out the door. He marched down their lane to the road without even seeing me. I waited a while, hoping no one in there was injured, and then I heard Emily and Laura talking, so I figured they were all right. I decided to follow Bert and have it out with him, right in the road if necessary. He was well ahead of me, though. When I got down the lane and looked around I could see in the dying light that he was running toward the ruins, swerving about. He looked drunk to me—that or out of his senses. Both, as it turned out." Mom's jaw set.

When she continued, her voice was scratchy. "He saw me when he reached the Deserted Village. He leaned against a ruin and watched me climb toward him. When I got there, he lunged and pulled me down, and I rolled over the sill into the ruin. The rocks on the ground dug into my back. The bastard straddled me like a rapist, and I screamed, the way they told us to in school: if a man attacks you, scream as hard as you can. He shut me up, though. He took me by the neck and started choking me. I was fighting for my breath and trying to pull his hands apart, when all at once he let go and he fell on top of me, weighing me down. I think I passed out for a minute. When I woke up, Emily was tugging at Bert's shoulders. She dragged him off me and let him fall to the ground. I sat up and saw the wound on the back of Bert's head and the bloody stone at his side. That's it. You know the rest."

"Challenging him took guts. You were courageous, Mom."

"Foolhardy is more like it. If Emily hadn't come, I'd be dead. The poor girl, she came to help him back to the house. He was drunk and raging. She'd seen him like that before, and so had Laura. They were afraid he'd pass out and spend the night in the cold, on the road or in some field."

"You mean she didn't follow him to attack him, to get revenge?"

Mom's lips pursed, and she looked at me disapprovingly. "You're too old to not know about drunks and abuse. She's the child of an alcoholic—well, the stepchild, the step*daughter*. It's the old story. He abuses her mother, he abuses her, and she protects him. She loves him." Mom's voice cracked.

"Are you telling me that Bert abused Emily?"

Mom sighed with exasperation. "Not sexual abuse. Not that. He did what he did to Laura—treated her like she was stupid, undercut her, controlled her, got drunk and raged, and hit her sometimes too. Laura hid it all at home and with their friends; she played the pampered wife. Emily had the job of hiding it at work; she cleaned up after him and the mistakes he made when he was drinking. If she had bruises that she couldn't conceal, she worked from home."

"When did you find this out, Mom? Did you know for years?"

"No. I began to sense it at the Jubilee. And then after Emily hit and killed him, she broke down and let me know everything. I walked her home, and we told Laura what had happened. We left Bert in the Deserted Village. There was nothing anyone could do for him. We were horrified, but we decided together to leave him where he was. We made a plan that I would protect Emily. I'd start by denying I was there, but if necessary I'd admit it. I would never, ever, mention Emily."

"How could you promise that? You could have spent your life in prison, all for the sake of . . ."

"A wounded girl. A victim. A victim of *that man*." Mom looked at me with defiance.

I swallowed hard and said, "I'm proud of you, Mom."

She put her hand on my cheek and said, "You're lovely." Her mother, my Portuguese grandma, says that. She means "I love you," but she never says those words. Instead, she says, "You're lovely." Is it a mistranslation? Or is she afraid that if she declares her love she'll lose it? Maybe that's what's behind Mom's habitual terseness. Best not to name the most precious feelings. Best that the spirits not know whom we love.

Dad's way is different. Most of the time he plays "the quiet man," but when asked he speaks his truth, emotional or not. After lunch in the kitchen, I lured him out onto the patio for a seat in the sun. Like Dad (the only one in the family who's as pale as me), I hid my eyes behind coal-black sunglasses and my face under a hiker's broad-brimmed hat. That was good cover, in more ways than one.

"Dad," I said, "I'm sorry about Uncle Bert." His head cocked, but he kept looking at the long slope toward the beach.

"I'm sorry you lost him." I was thinking how I would feel if I lost my brother, but Dad didn't give me time to think that out.

"I didn't *lose* him," he said gruffly.

What did that mean? I made a hasty guess.

"No, of course you didn't. He'll always be with you, really."

"Oh, come on. Cut the crap." I jumped in my seat.

"I'm sorry, Dad. I didn't mean to . . ."

"Stop saying you're sorry. You didn't kill him. Mom didn't kill him either. Bert provoked and corrupted people who got close to him. He brought out their greed and their ruthlessness. Someone was going to lash out at him eventually. It was your cousin's bad luck that she was the one. It could have been Laura. It could have been Mom."

I stopped breathing.

Dad's head turned, and he took off his sunglasses. He said, "Look at me, Nora." I did, and I removed my glasses too.

"I know you thought it was Mom."

My silence was my confession.

"It's okay," Dad said. "You get your view of human nature from me. Anyone is capable of murder. Even people you love. It takes civilizing and self-discipline and fortunate circumstances to keep us from doing our worst. I could have been like Bert, and you could have been like Emily."

"No, I couldn't. I didn't have Bert for a father; I had you."

He said wryly, "I call that a fortunate circumstance. But it's a miracle that you have Mom. She's the strongest woman I know."

"And the most loyal."

"You're pretty much a carbon copy, you know."

I smiled at the irony—me, as loyal as Mom. I just said, "People don't say 'carbon copy' anymore, Dad. Nobody knows what that is."

"What would they say then? You're a Xerox copy of her?"

"That doesn't work either. But I'm glad you think I'm like Mom. I'd like to be."

"I'll pray you'll have 'fortunate circumstances' too."

"I'll consider that my father's blessing."

"You do that," he said, rising to his feet. He kissed the rough canvas of my hatted head.

Epilogue

IT WAS DAD'S IDEA to take the family out to dinner the following night as a way of welcoming Sister Bridget, who had arrived from Galway early in the morning to offer what help she could. She certainly proved her worth. Bridget comforted Aunt Laura and prayed with her at the jail, where Emily was in custody. She "had a word" with Inspector O'Donnell, who decided afterward not to press charges against Mom for withholding information. (It seems that "little Kevin O'Donnell" had been a pupil of Sister Bridget's when she taught parochial school on Achill years ago, and he was still in awe of her.) And Bridget supported Angie when she announced at lunch that she was moving in with her new boyfriend instead of going home.

Angie asked if she could invite Bobby to the dinner. I thought of including Maggie but she had a date—not with Declan, who was now relegated to the category of definite ex, but with Sean, the doorman at the Achill Arms. It was just as well they couldn't come. Explaining to

Sister Bridget how they met would have been awkward. Maggie's plan was to return to her boyfriend in France, but until then, well, Maggie was Maggie.

Our group arrived at Masterson's Pub and stood outside for a while, gazing over the strand into a wispy sunset. Once through the door, we were ushered to a raised dining area up a few steps across from the bar. We took over the small space, which had just two booths. Toby and I shared one with Angie and Bobby, while Mom, Dad, Aunt Laura, and Sister Bridget took the other.

Over fish and chips, I prodded Angie about her announcement that she was not going back home, neither to the convent at Grace Quarry nor to the beauty salon in Gloucester. She had found a new home on Achill Island. Though they were silly with love, Bobby and Angie had sensible plans. She would live at the farm with Bobby, his mother, and Blackie. Mrs. Colman, considerably older than our mom, suffered from arthritis and would be glad to have the help of a strong young woman whom she welcomed as a daughter. Already Angie referred to her as Mam, as Bobby did. I could have seen it all as alarmingly swift, but I liked Bobby and for the first time I trusted Angie's instincts about her man.

It reassured me to hear that Angie and Bobby had confided in Sister Bridget and sought her guidance. Bridget believed in female self-sufficiency, and she was cautious about Angie becoming the third hand on the farm, at least right away. It might be better to find a job on the island—cutting hair, maybe—and take time to test whether she loved sheep-tending as much as she loved Bobby. Angie is resourceful and flexible. I had faith that she would find her way on Achill, especially with the help of Sister Bridget, Bobby, his family, and the friends she had made while acting in *The Playboy of the Western World.*

"I've been thinking about that play," I said. "What happens at the end? I never got to see it. I bet Christy gets the girl and somehow or other it all works out."

"That's what I expected too," said Angie, "but it doesn't happen. When the crowd sees Christy clobber his father right in front of their eyes, they turn against him, even Pegeen. She says it's one thing to hear about a terrible deed, another thing to see it take place in your own backyard."

"What happens to the father?" I asked. "Has Christy really killed him?"

"Everyone thinks so," said Bobby, "but no, he crawls back in, in a daze. In the end, Christy and his father go off together, but things have changed between them. From now on, Christy will be the boss."

"What about Pegeen?" I asked. I didn't want her left alone.

"That dope Shawn Keogh says, well, now we can get married, after all, but she slaps him in the face." Bobby smacked the air in front of Toby's nose.

"She wants Christy back," said Angie. "But it's too late. He can't forgive her for turning against him. The play ends with her wailing, 'Oh my grief, I've lost him surely. I've lost the only Playboy of the Western World.'"

"It's a sad ending for a comedy," observed Toby.

"It is," Bobby agreed. "I think Synge was ribbing us about our blasted blarney. He got a laugh out of our love of wild talk, but in the end he stuck it to us. If we let ourselves get snookered by the grand talkers among us, we'll never get on in the world."

"That's as may be," said Angie, slipping her arm through Bobby's. "I'm not going to make the same mistake Pegeen did. I'm not letting *my* playboy get away."

"Me neither," I said.

Angie and I clinked beer mugs, and the guys raised theirs to each other.

After dinner Toby and I excused ourselves and slipped out for what would be our last walk along the beach. By then the sun had sunk behind Mount Slievemore. The breeze carried a chill, and I shivered. "You all right?" Toby asked.

"A little cold," I said.

"Here, take my jacket. It's warmer than yours." He insisted. He was wearing a bulky Irish knit sweater underneath. I put on his jacket gratefully and carried my thinner rain jacket over my arm.

"How's the ankle?"

"Better," I said. "As long as we don't walk too fast."

He slowed the pace. "I'm ready to go home. How about you?"

"I guess so."

He stopped, put both hands on my shoulders, and studied my face. "Something's still bothering you. What is it?"

I shrugged.

"I know you're worried about Emily, but Angie's got a boyfriend and your mom's in the clear. Things are looking up, no?"

"It's just that I feel bad about not being straight with Mom, not telling her about the button I found, and thinking she was guilty of murdering Uncle Bert."

"Now that it's over, you could tell her, I suppose." He took my hand and we continued walking, slowly.

"She'd think I wasn't loyal. I couldn't handle that."

"Okay, that I understand." We continued for a while without talking. Then Toby asked, "What would you have done if the case had dragged on or never been solved?"

"I don't know. I've been asking myself that question, and I just don't know. I wish I'd never found that damned button."

"Your mom never missed it?"

"Sure she did. She brought the sweater in to Sweeney's Woolen Shop to get all the buttons replaced. The sweater was there the day the detectives searched the cottage, which is why they never found any hard evidence against her.

"Where is it, by the way?" asked Toby.

"The button? In my pocket. I've been carrying it with me all along. I couldn't think of a safer hiding place unless I was subject to a strip search, and that was unlikely. Now it just reminds me of my dilemma. Do you turn in your own mother if you suspect her of a crime, or do you become complicit by keeping her secret?"

"It's a hard question, all right," said Toby.

"What's the answer?"

“May I see it?”

I dug into the pocket of my jeans and pulled out the button. Toby weighed it carefully in his hand. Then he broke into a trot toward the verge of the water. With the tide lapping his shoes, he drew back his arm and threw the button as far as he could, high into the air, into the sea.

Acknowledgments

We are deeply grateful to our cousin Sister Riona McHugh for welcoming us into her extended family and for introducing us to Achill Island. Thanks also to Father Kieran McHugh for suggesting a plot idea related to Irish lore. Our friend JoAnn Skloot shared information we could not have obtained elsewhere. Garda Martin O'Reilly (Achill Sound, County Mayo) and Garda John McNamara (Westport Garda Station) generously spent time with us explaining police procedures and jurisdictional issues pertaining to crime on Achill Island. We also thank John McGinty of Galway for useful historical facts and Kieran Sweeney for information on performances at Achill Sound Town Hall.

We used the following books for background: Heinrich Boll, *Irish Journal* (Brooklyn, NY: Melville House Printing, 2011); Theresa McDonald, *Achill Island: Archeology, History, Folklore* (St. O'Hara's Hill, Tullamore: L.A.S. Publications, 2006); Jonathan Beaumont, *Rails to Achill: A West of Ireland Branch Line* (Usk, Wales: Oakwood Press, 2005); S. B. Kennedy, *Paul Henry* (New Haven, CT: National Gallery of Ireland and Yale University Press, 2003); Patricia Byrne, *The Veiled Woman of Achill: Island Outrage & a Playboy Drama* (Cork: Collins Press, 2012).

Thanks again to the dedicated staff at the University of Wisconsin Press. Publication of this book occurs shortly after the retirement of three key people: our editor, Raphael Kadushin, who coaxed five books out of us; Sheila Leary, who managed publicity and events; and Andrea Christofferson, responsible for marketing and sales. Behind the scenes, Scott Lenz and TG Design designed the interior pages and book covers that felt just right for the series. Editing and production was overseen by Sheila McMahon, and copyediting was done by Michelle Wing. We are deeply grateful to all for their care and creativity.

Finally, there's nothing so valuable as a critical reading by a friend and fellow author. Thank you, Kim Hays.

Books by Betsy Draine and Michael Hinden

A NORA BARNES AND TOBY SANDLER MYSTERY

Murder in Lascaux

The Body in Bodega Bay

Death on a Starry Night

A Castle in the Backyard: The Dream of a House in France

The Walnut Cookbook by Jean-Luc Toussaint (translators and editors)

BETSY DRAINE AND MICHAEL HINDEN are emeritus professors of English at the University of Wisconsin–Madison and the co-authors of the Nora Barnes and Toby Sandler mystery series. Their first collaboration was a memoir, *A Castle in the Backyard: The Dream of a House in France* (2002), inspired by their twenty summers in the Dordogne in southwest France.

Michael Hinden won a Kiekhofer Award for Excellence in Teaching in 1972 and was named Bascom Professor of Integrated Liberal Studies in 2004. At the University of Wisconsin–Madison, he taught modern drama in the Department of English and literature and the arts in the Integrated Liberal Studies Program. He chaired the ILS Program from 1981 to 1984 and served as Associate Dean of International Studies from 1991 to 2003. His publications include *Long Day's Journey into Night: Native Eloquence* (1990).

Betsy Draine served as Chair of Women's Studies (1989–92) and Vice Provost for Academic Affairs (1992–99) at the University of Wisconsin–Madison. The focus of her administrative work was on gender equity and work climate. She taught courses in modern British fiction and is the author of *Substance under Pressure: Artistic Coherence and Evolving Form in the Novels of Doris Lessing* (1983). She won the 1990 Chancellor's Award for Excellence in Teaching and the 2002 Phi Beta Kappa Teaching Award. Betsy and Michael retired in 2005.